SUPER POTATO

#8 SUPER POTATO AND THE SOARING TERROR OF THE PTEROSAUR

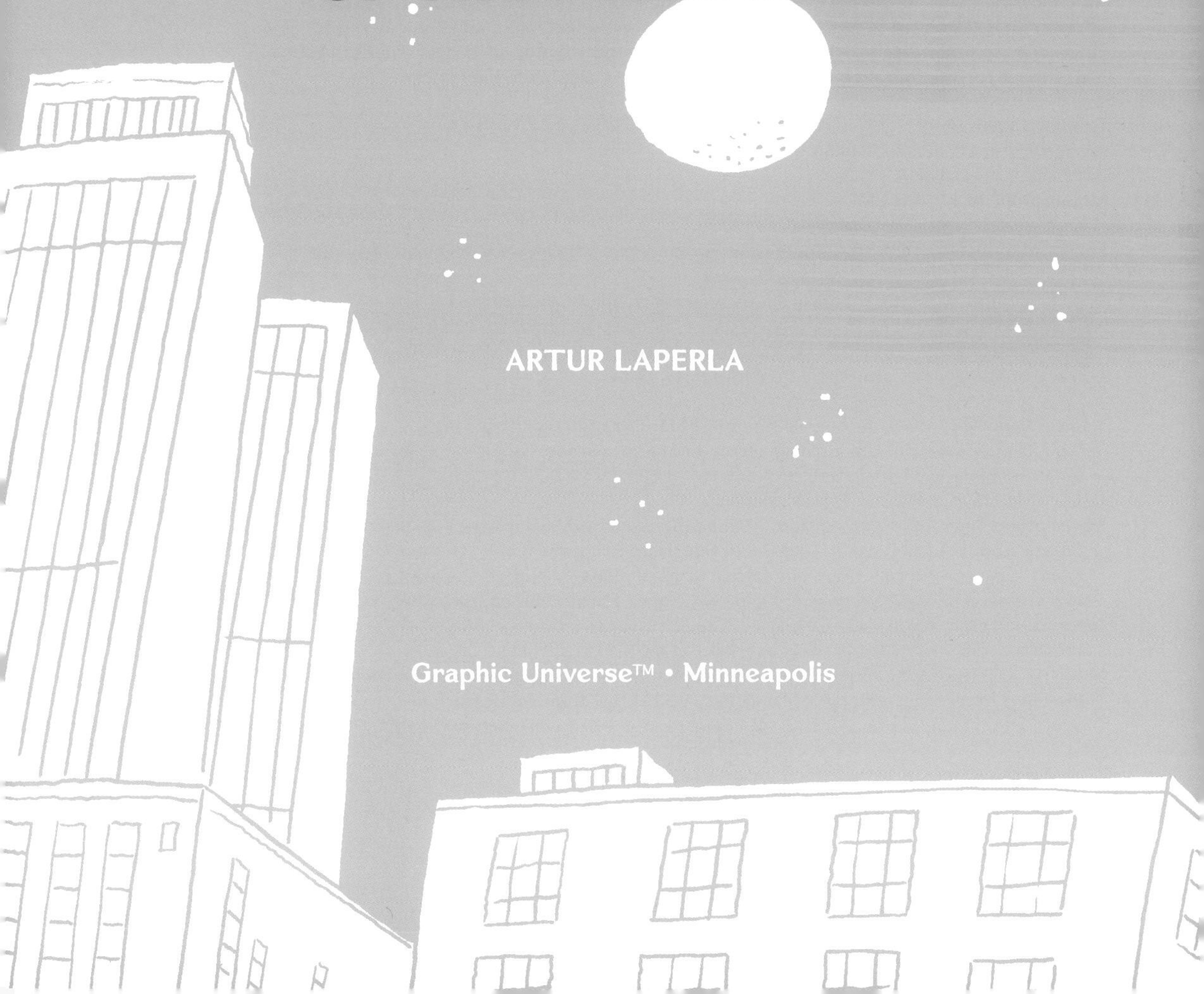

ARTUR LAPERLA

Graphic Universe™ • Minneapolis

Story and illustrations by Artur Laperla
Translation by Norwyn MacTíre

First American edition published in 2022 by Graphic Universe™

Graphic Universe™
An imprint of Lerner Publishing Group, Inc.
241 First Avenue North
Minneapolis, MN 55401 USA

For reading levels and more information, look up this title at www.lernerbooks.com.

Main body text set in CCWildWords. Typeface provided by Comicraft.

Library of Congress Cataloging-in-Publication Data

Names: Laperla (Artist), author, illustrator. | MacTire, Norwyn, translator.
Title: Super Potato and the soaring terror of the pterosaur : book 8 / story and illustrations by Artur Laperla ; translation by Norwyn MacTíre.
Other titles: Super Patata (Series). English
Description: First American edition. | Minneapolis : Graphic Universe , 2022. | Series: Super Potato ; book 8 | Audience: Ages 7–11 | Summary: Augusta Richly, the world's richest girl, wants a pterosaur, but when her father hires a villainous super-scientist to make it happen, the prehistoric creature escapes and only Super Potato can capture the winged lizard.
Identifiers: LCCN 2021014437 (print) | LCCN 2021014438 (ebook) | ISBN 9781728424583 (library binding) | ISBN 9781728448749 (paperback) | ISBN 9781728444161 (ebook)
Subjects: LCSH: Graphic novels. | CYAC: Graphic novels. | Superheroes—Fiction. | Potatoes—Fiction. | Pterosaurs—Fiction. | Dinosaurs—Fiction. | Humorous stories.
Classification: LCC PZ7.7.L367 St 2022 (print) | LCC PZ7.7.L367 (ebook) | DDC 741.5/973—dc23

LC record available at https://lccn.loc.gov/2021014437
LC ebook record available at https://lccn.loc.gov/2021014438

Manufactured in the United States of America
1-49327-49443-6/28/2021

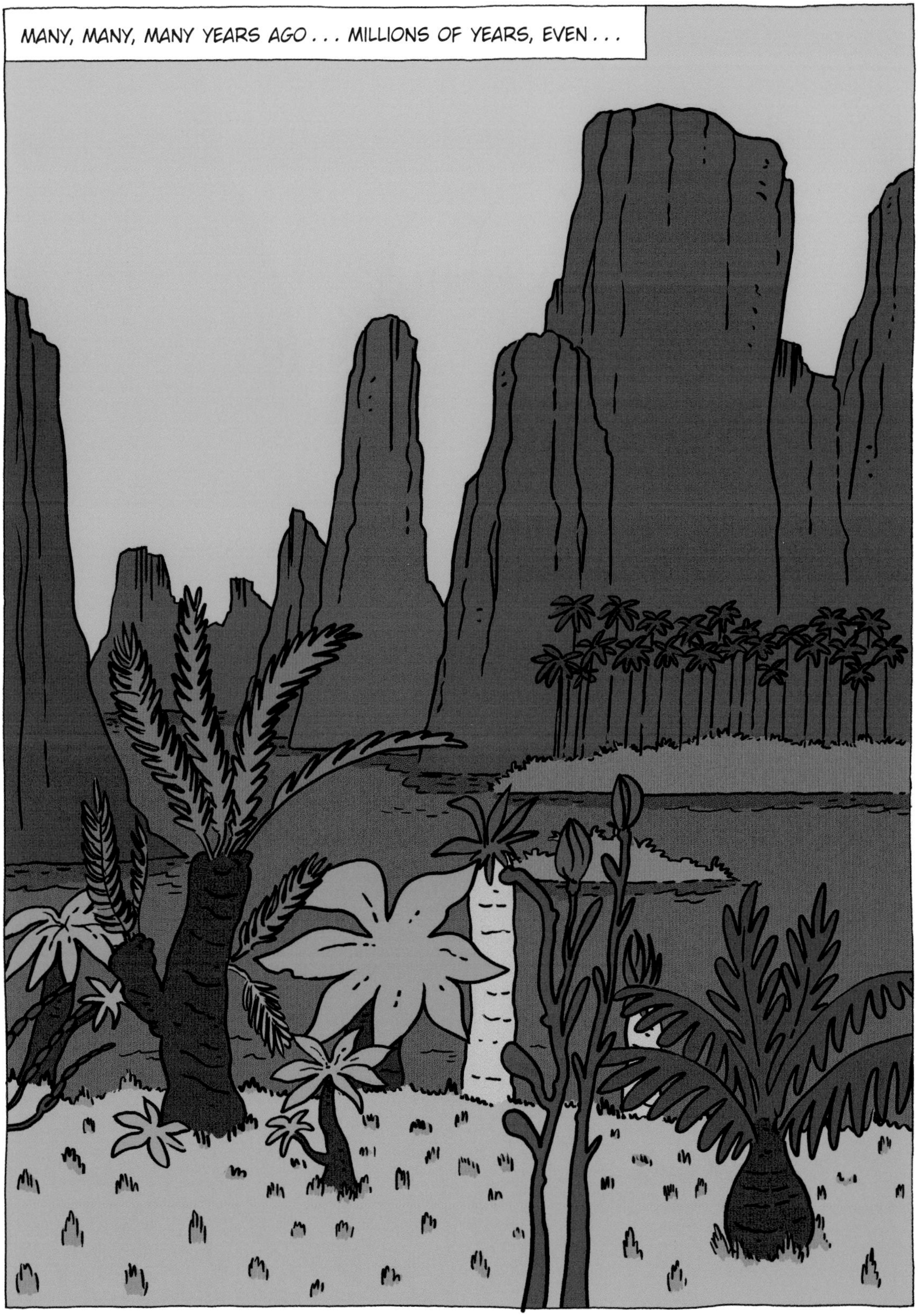
MANY, MANY, MANY YEARS AGO . . . MILLIONS OF YEARS, EVEN . . .

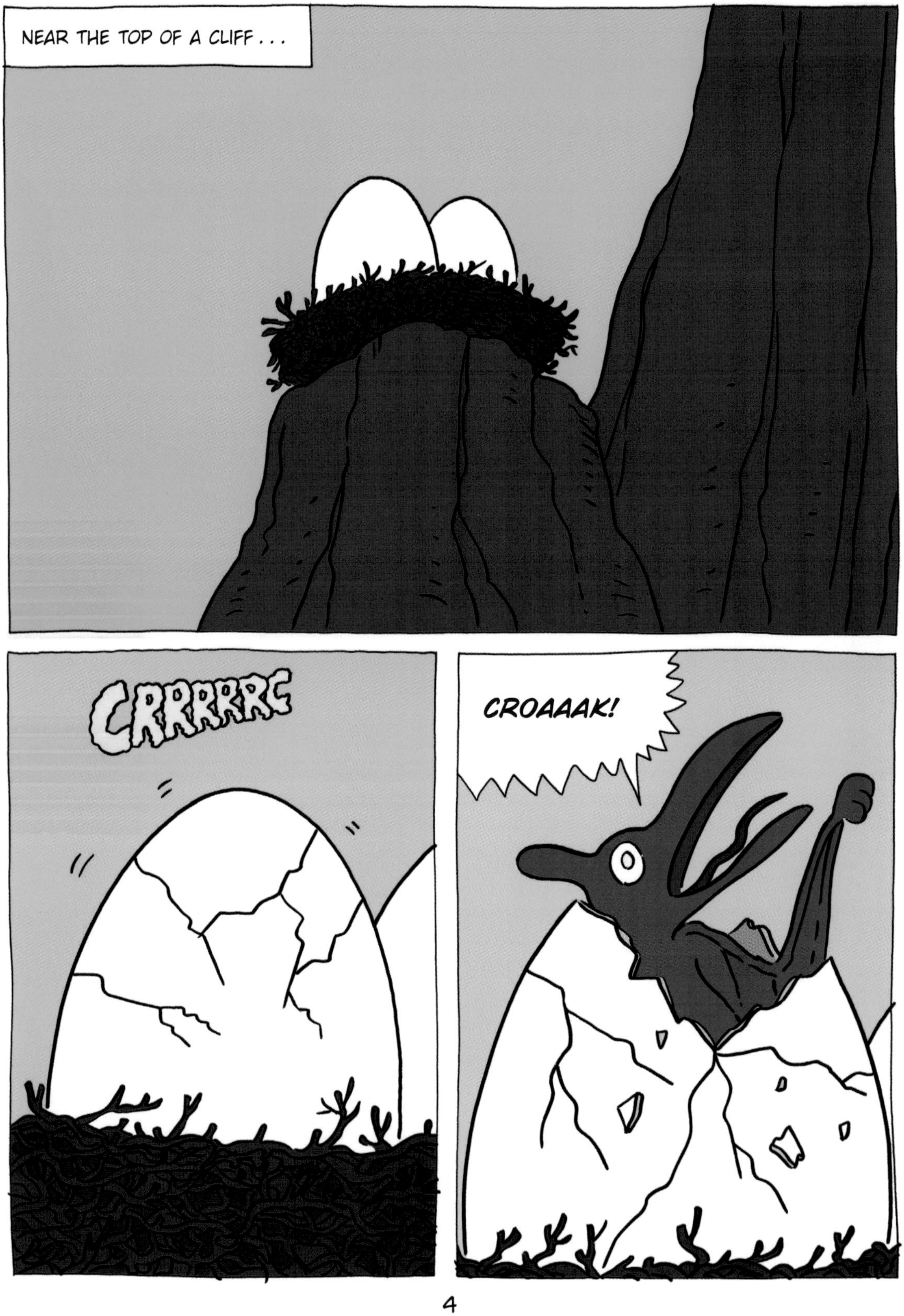
NEAR THE TOP OF A CLIFF . . .
CRRRRRC
CROAAAK!

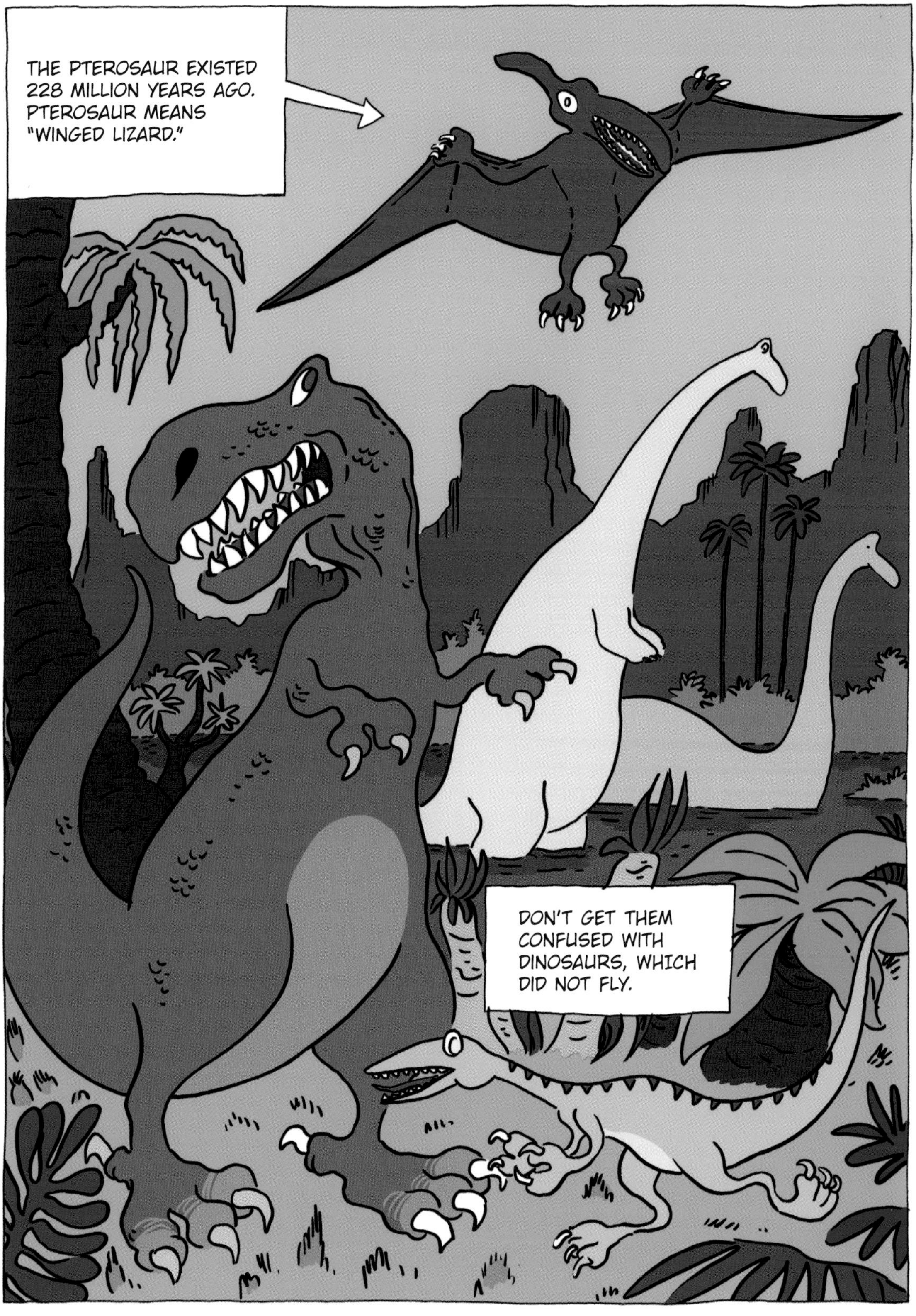
THE PTEROSAUR EXISTED 228 MILLION YEARS AGO. PTEROSAUR MEANS "WINGED LIZARD."
DON'T GET THEM CONFUSED WITH DINOSAURS, WHICH DID NOT FLY.

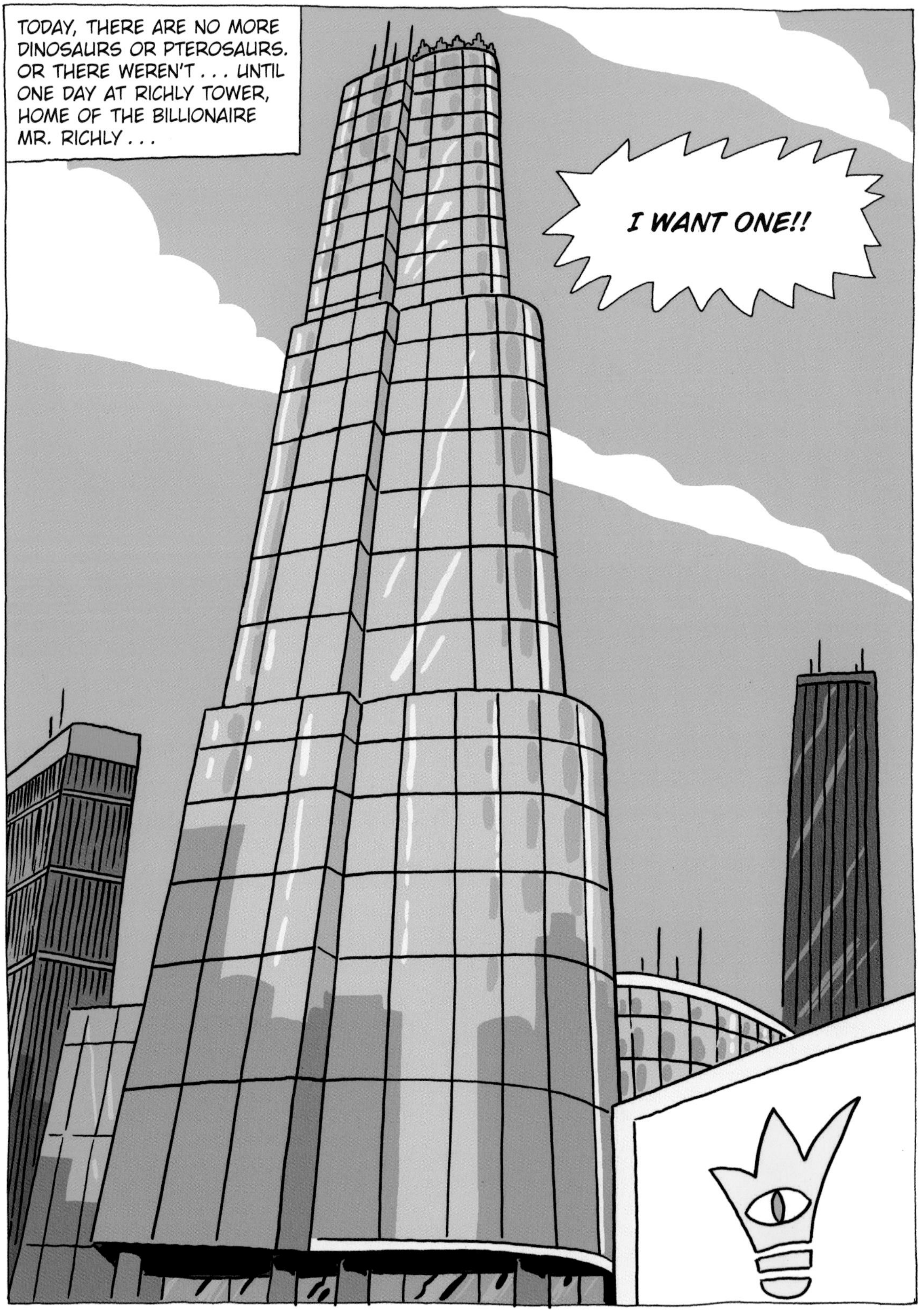
TODAY, THERE ARE NO MORE DINOSAURS OR PTEROSAURS. OR THERE WEREN'T . . . UNTIL ONE DAY AT RICHLY TOWER, HOME OF THE BILLIONAIRE MR. RICHLY . . .
I WANT ONE!!

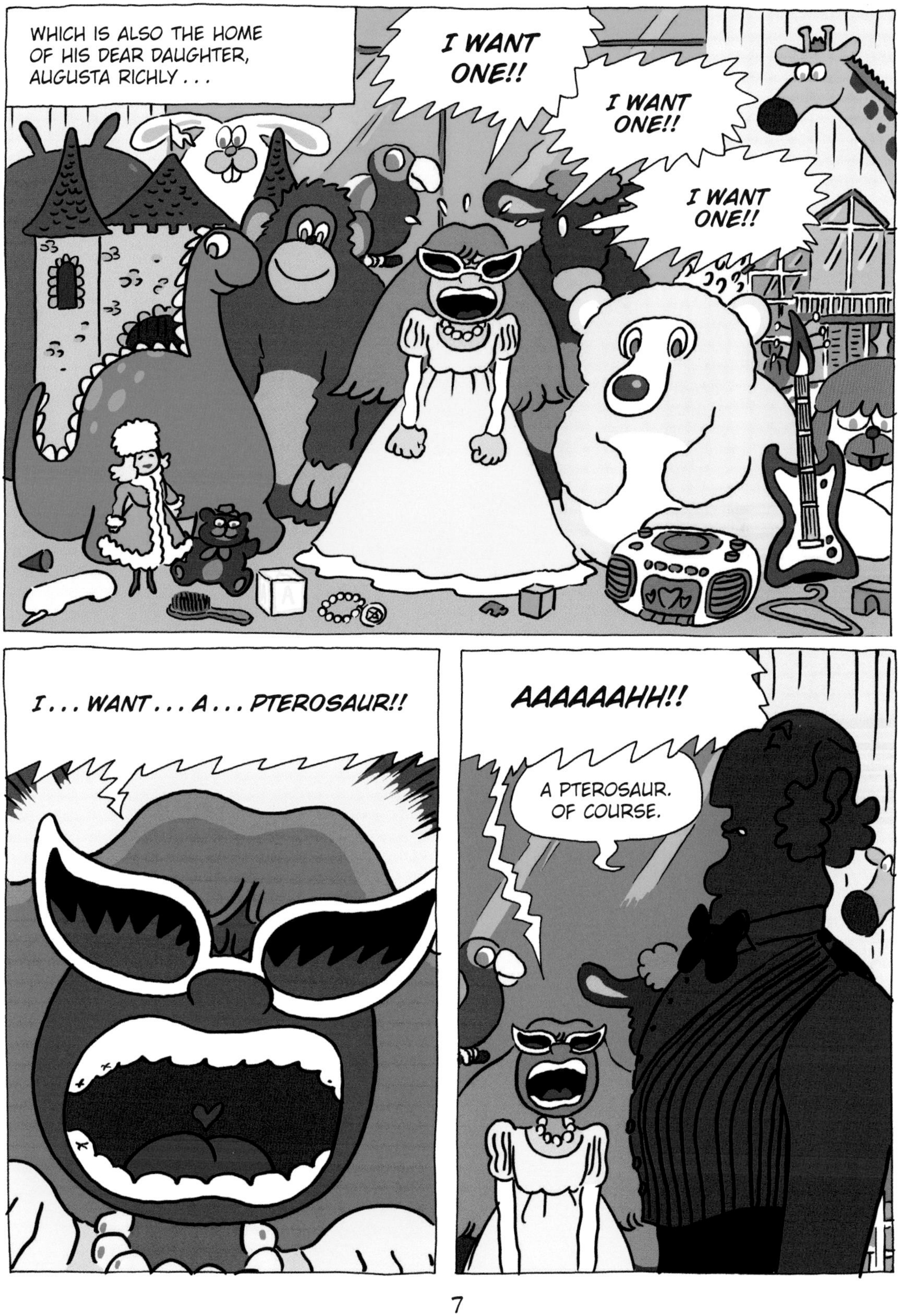
WHICH IS ALSO THE HOME OF HIS DEAR DAUGHTER, AUGUSTA RICHLY . . .
I WANT ONE!!
I WANT ONE!!
I WANT ONE!!
I . . . WANT . . . A . . . PTEROSAUR!!
AAAAAAHH!!
A PTEROSAUR. OF COURSE.

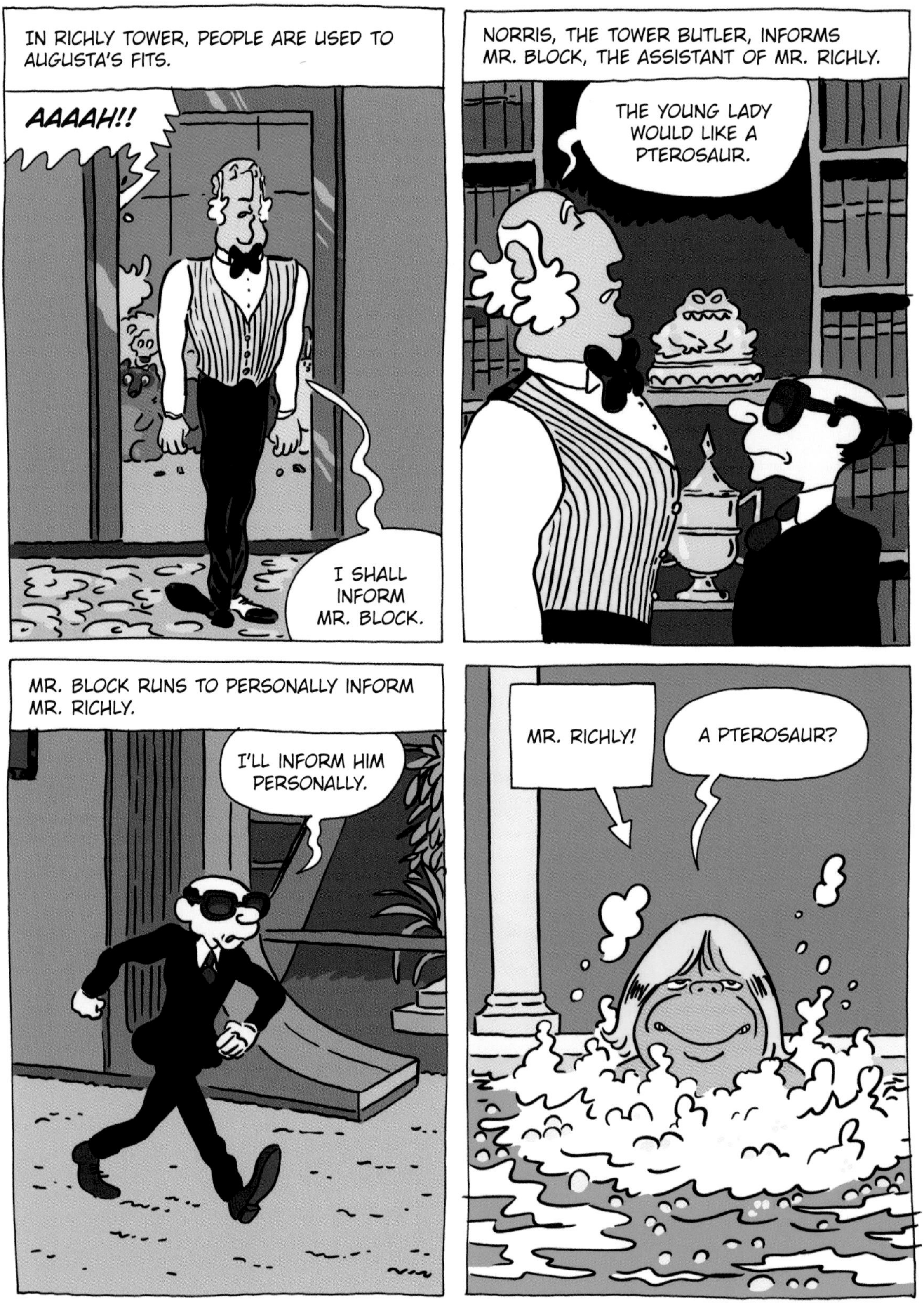
IN RICHLY TOWER, PEOPLE ARE USED TO AUGUSTA'S FITS.
AAAAH!!
I SHALL INFORM MR. BLOCK.
NORRIS, THE TOWER BUTLER, INFORMS MR. BLOCK, THE ASSISTANT OF MR. RICHLY.
THE YOUNG LADY WOULD LIKE A PTEROSAUR.
MR. BLOCK RUNS TO PERSONALLY INFORM MR. RICHLY.
I'LL INFORM HIM PERSONALLY.
MR. RICHLY!
A PTEROSAUR?

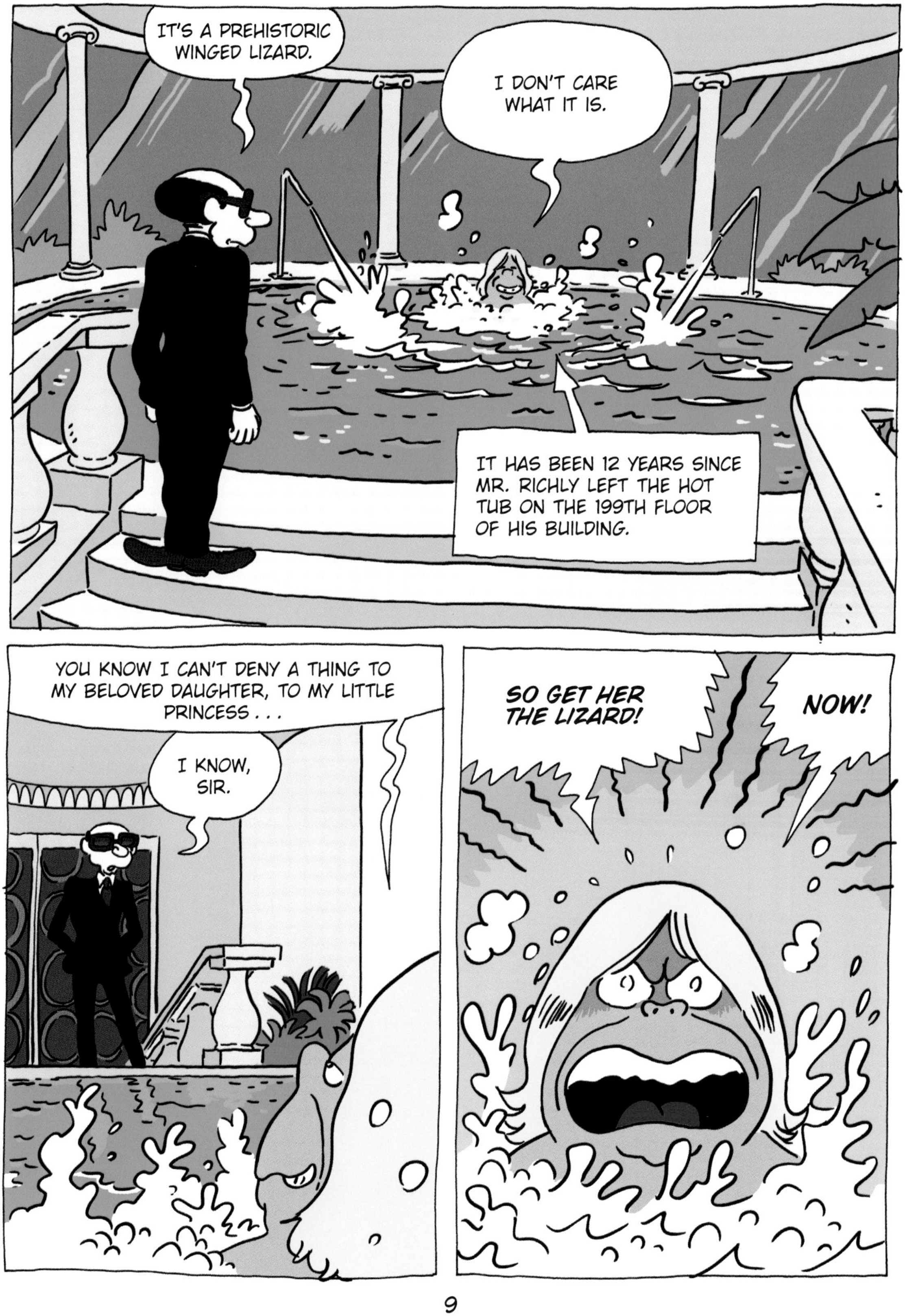
IT'S A PREHISTORIC WINGED LIZARD.
I DON'T CARE WHAT IT IS.
IT HAS BEEN 12 YEARS SINCE MR. RICHLY LEFT THE HOT TUB ON THE 199TH FLOOR OF HIS BUILDING.
YOU KNOW I CAN'T DENY A THING TO MY BELOVED DAUGHTER, TO MY LITTLE PRINCESS . . .
I KNOW, SIR.
SO GET HER THE LIZARD!
NOW!

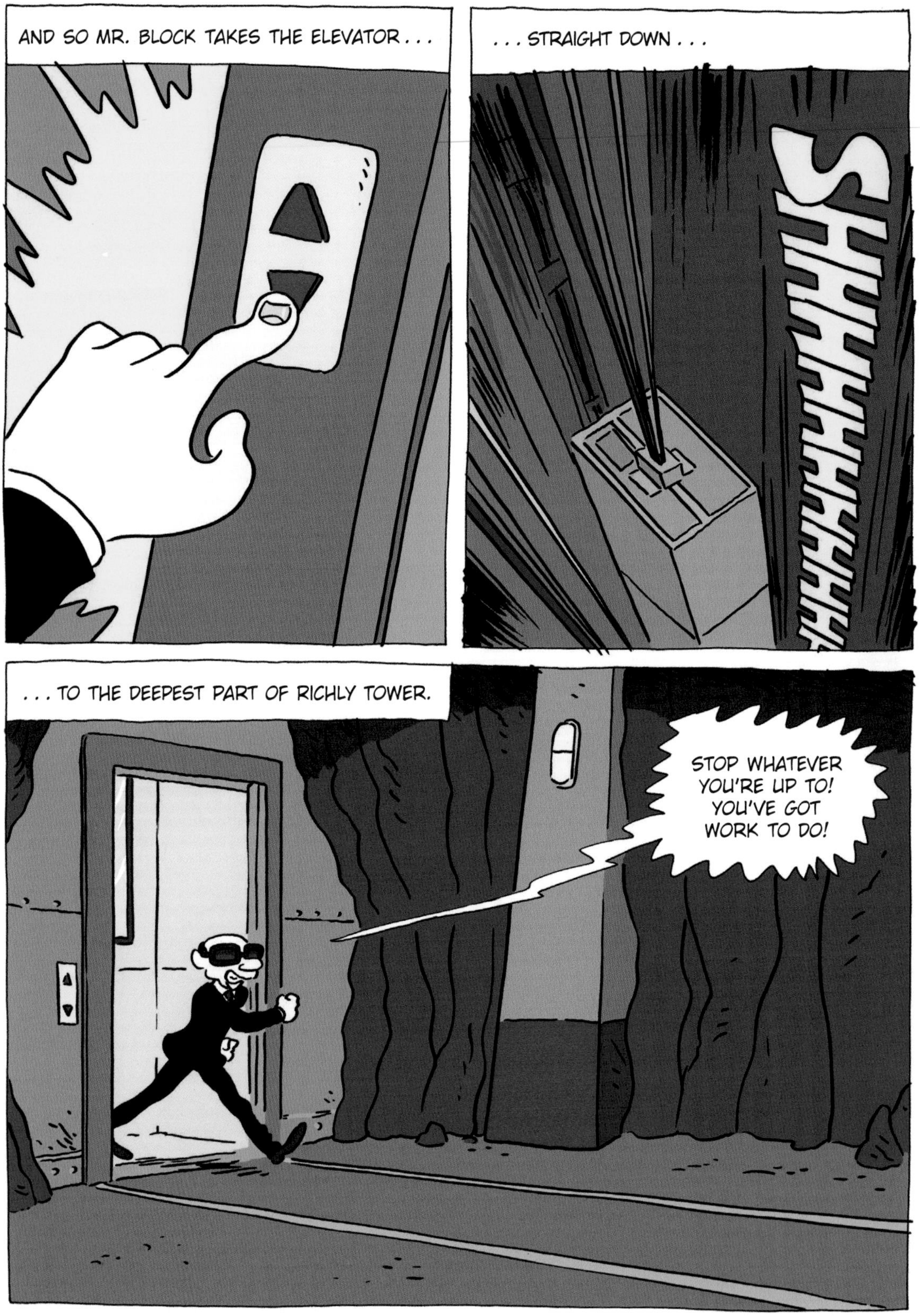
AND SO MR. BLOCK TAKES THE ELEVATOR . . .
. . . STRAIGHT DOWN . . .
SHHHHHHHHHHHHH
. . . TO THE DEEPEST PART OF RICHLY TOWER.
STOP WHATEVER YOU'RE UP TO! YOU'VE GOT WORK TO DO!

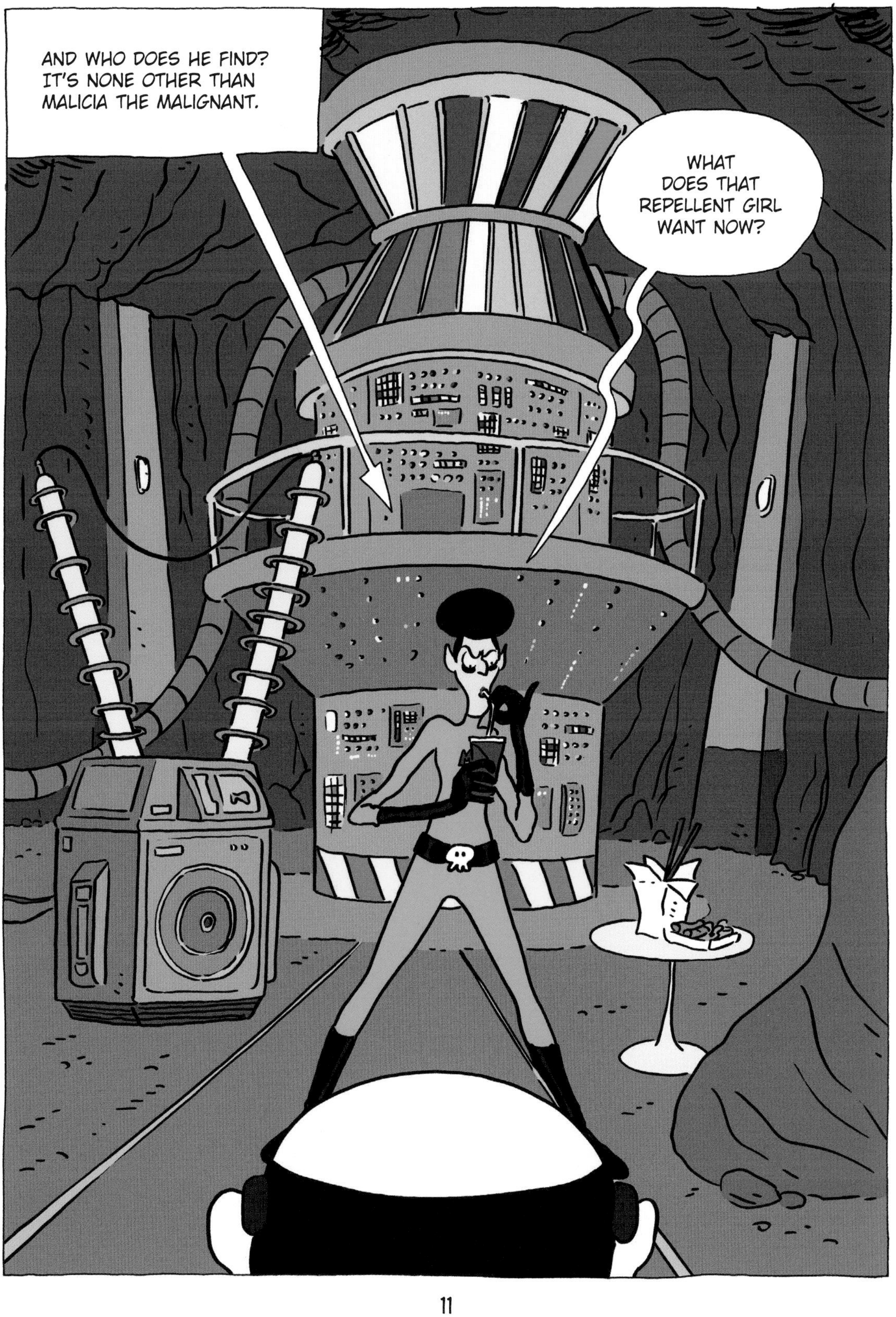
AND WHO DOES HE FIND? IT'S NONE OTHER THAN MALICIA THE MALIGNANT.
WHAT DOES THAT REPELLENT GIRL WANT NOW?

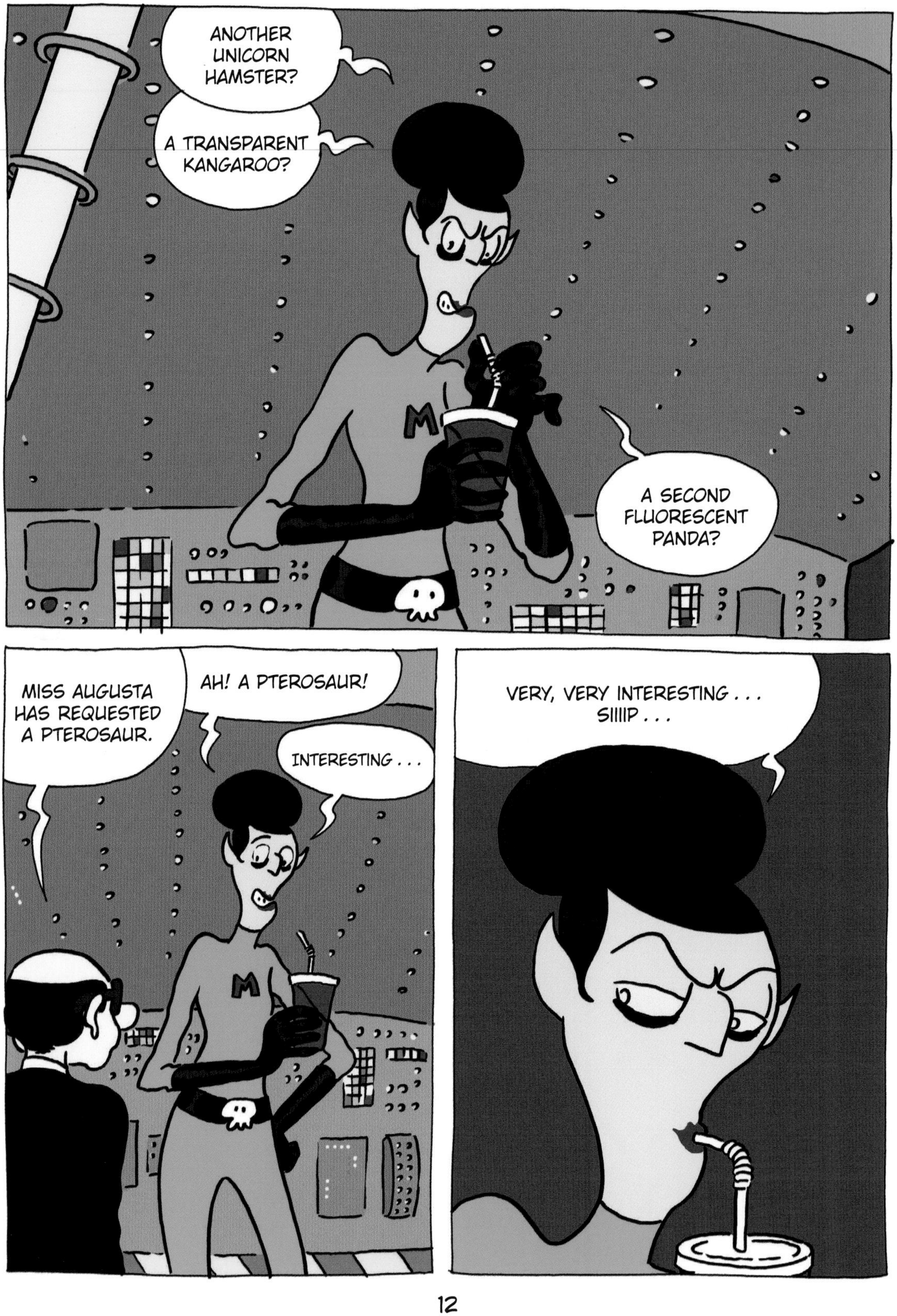
ANOTHER UNICORN HAMSTER?
A TRANSPARENT KANGAROO?
A SECOND FLUORESCENT PANDA?
MISS AUGUSTA HAS REQUESTED A PTEROSAUR.
AH! A PTEROSAUR!
INTERESTING . . .
VERY, VERY INTERESTING . . .
SIIIIP . . .

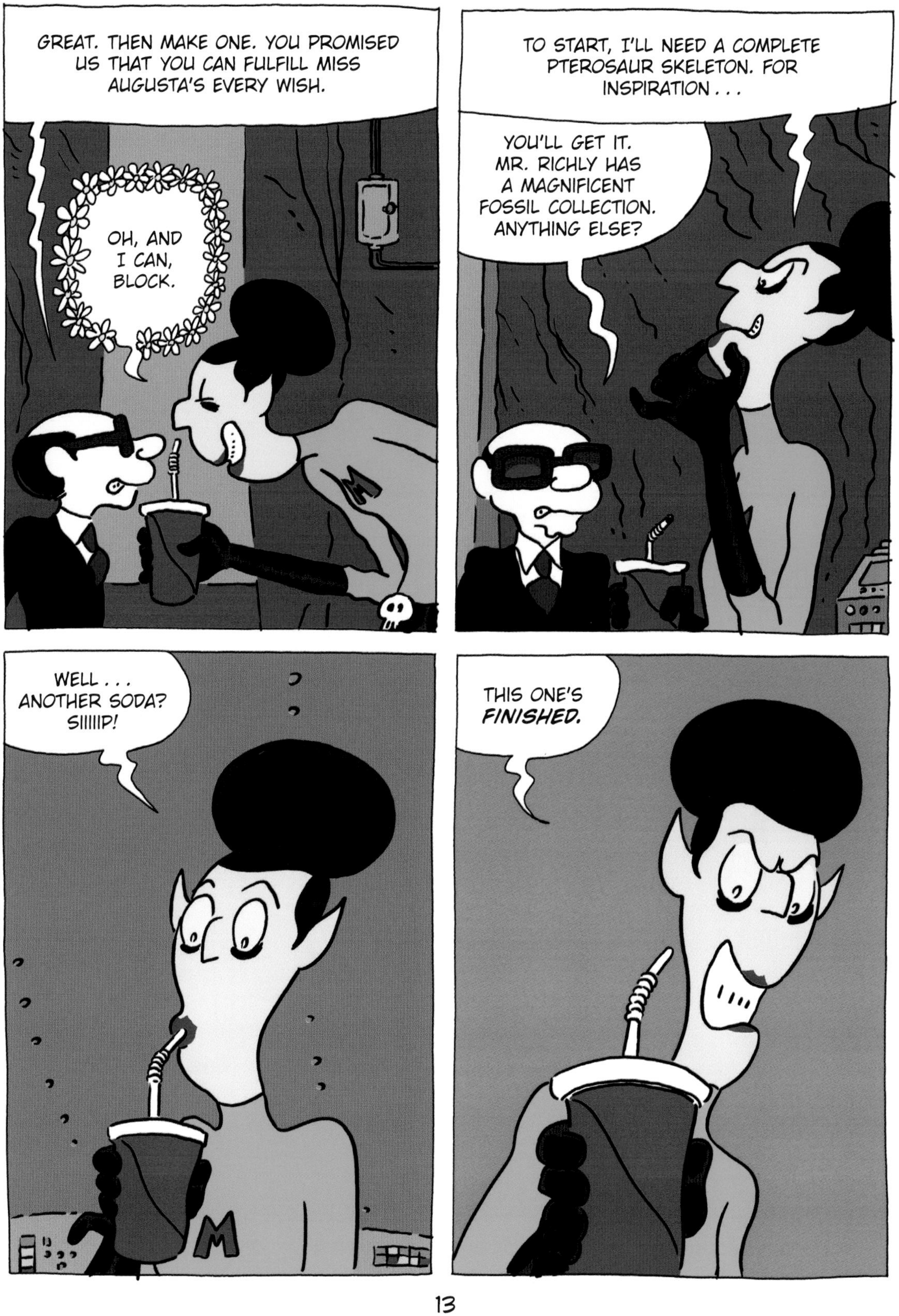
GREAT. THEN MAKE ONE. YOU PROMISED US THAT YOU CAN FULFILL MISS AUGUSTA'S EVERY WISH.
OH, AND I CAN, BLOCK.
TO START, I'LL NEED A COMPLETE PTEROSAUR SKELETON. FOR INSPIRATION . . .
YOU'LL GET IT. MR. RICHLY HAS A MAGNIFICENT FOSSIL COLLECTION. ANYTHING ELSE?
WELL . . . ANOTHER SODA? SIIIIIP!
THIS ONE'S ***FINISHED.***

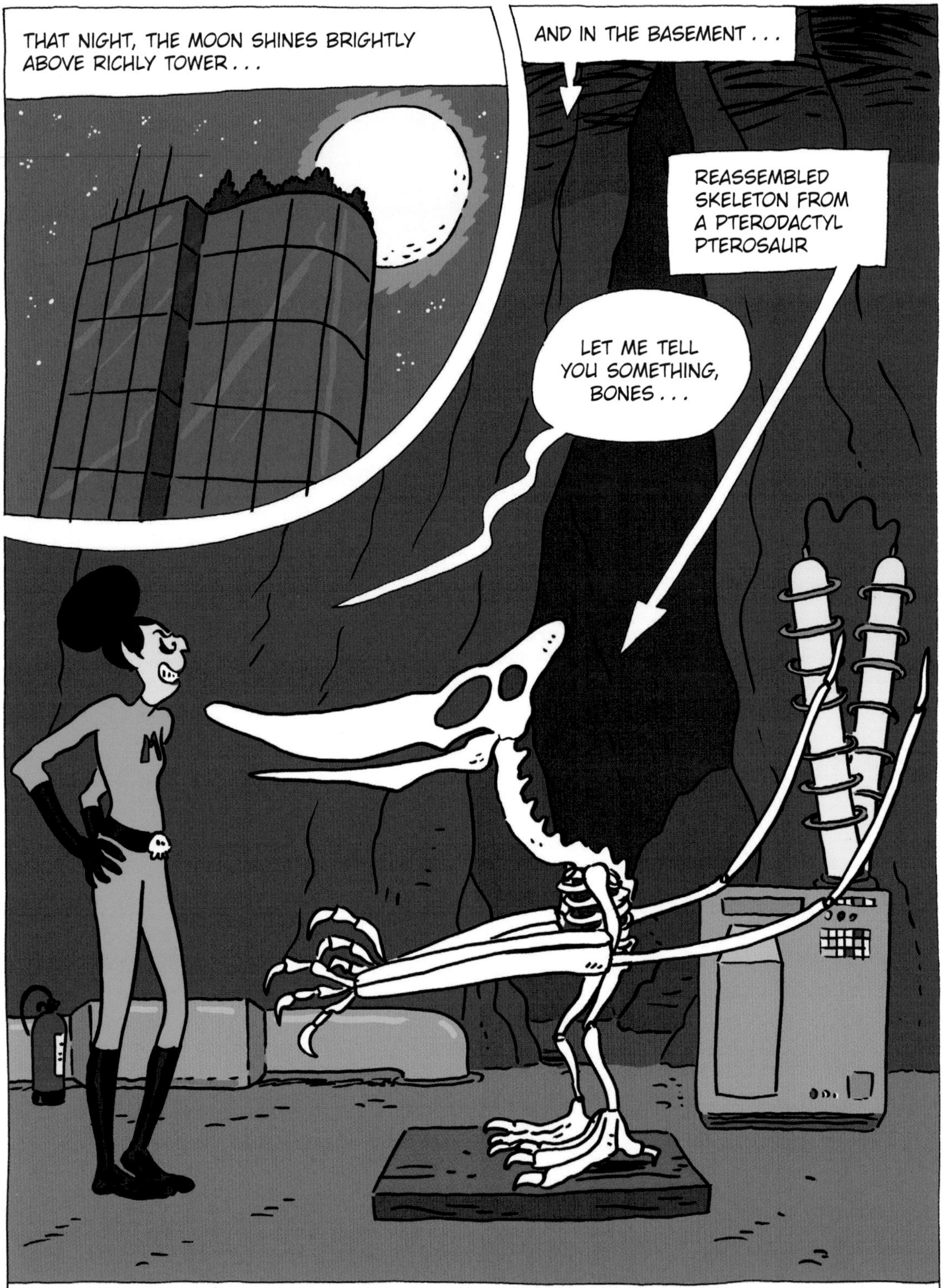
THAT NIGHT, THE MOON SHINES BRIGHTLY ABOVE RICHLY TOWER . . .
AND IN THE BASEMENT . . .
REASSEMBLED SKELETON FROM A PTERODACTYL PTEROSAUR
LET ME TELL YOU SOMETHING, BONES . . .
MALICIA THE MALIGNANT IS PREPARING TO RESURRECT A PREHISTORIC MONSTER.

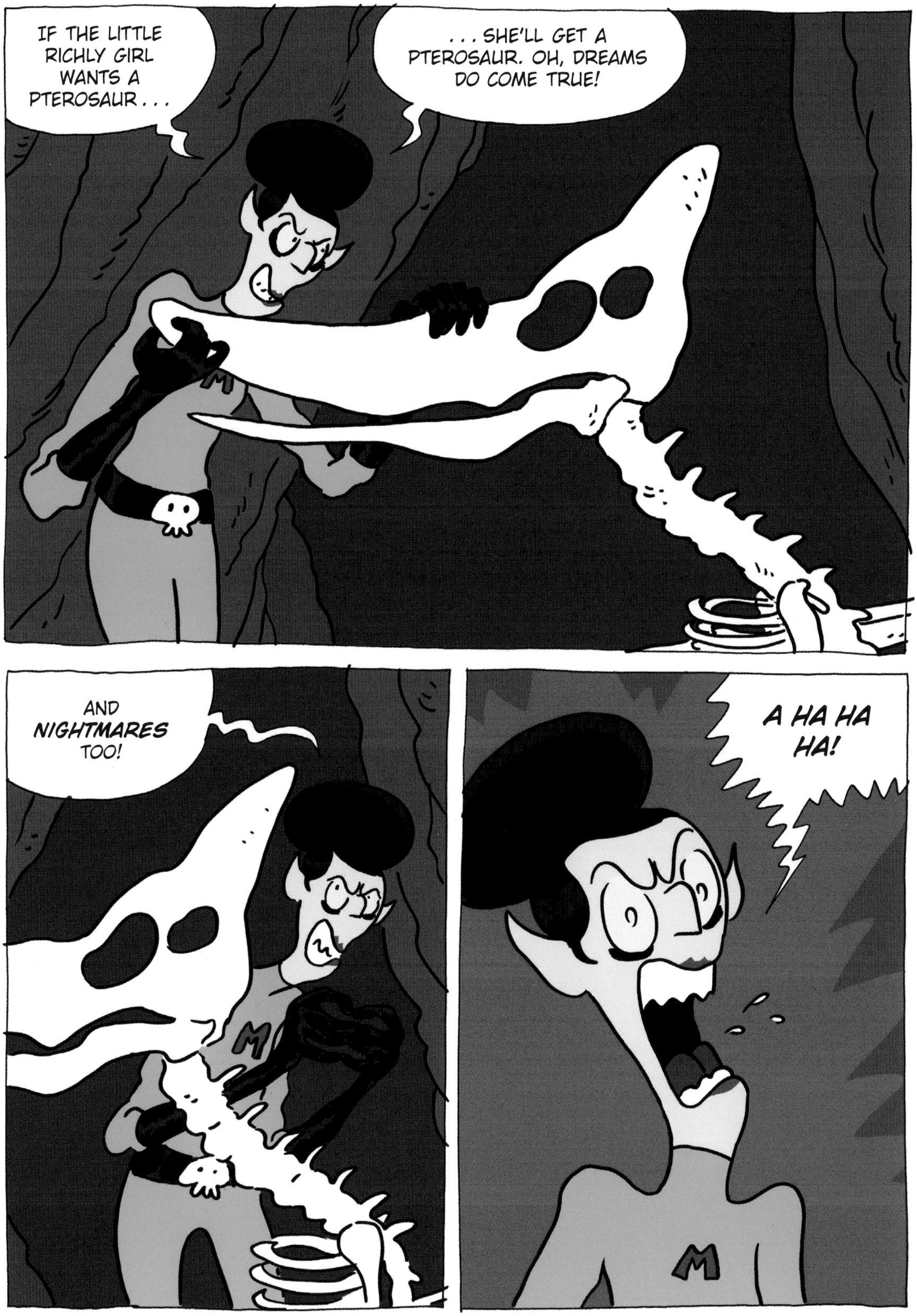
IF THE LITTLE RICHLY GIRL WANTS A PTEROSAUR . . .
. . . SHE'LL GET A PTEROSAUR. OH, DREAMS DO COME TRUE!
AND NIGHTMARES TOO!
A HA HA HA HA!
M
M
M

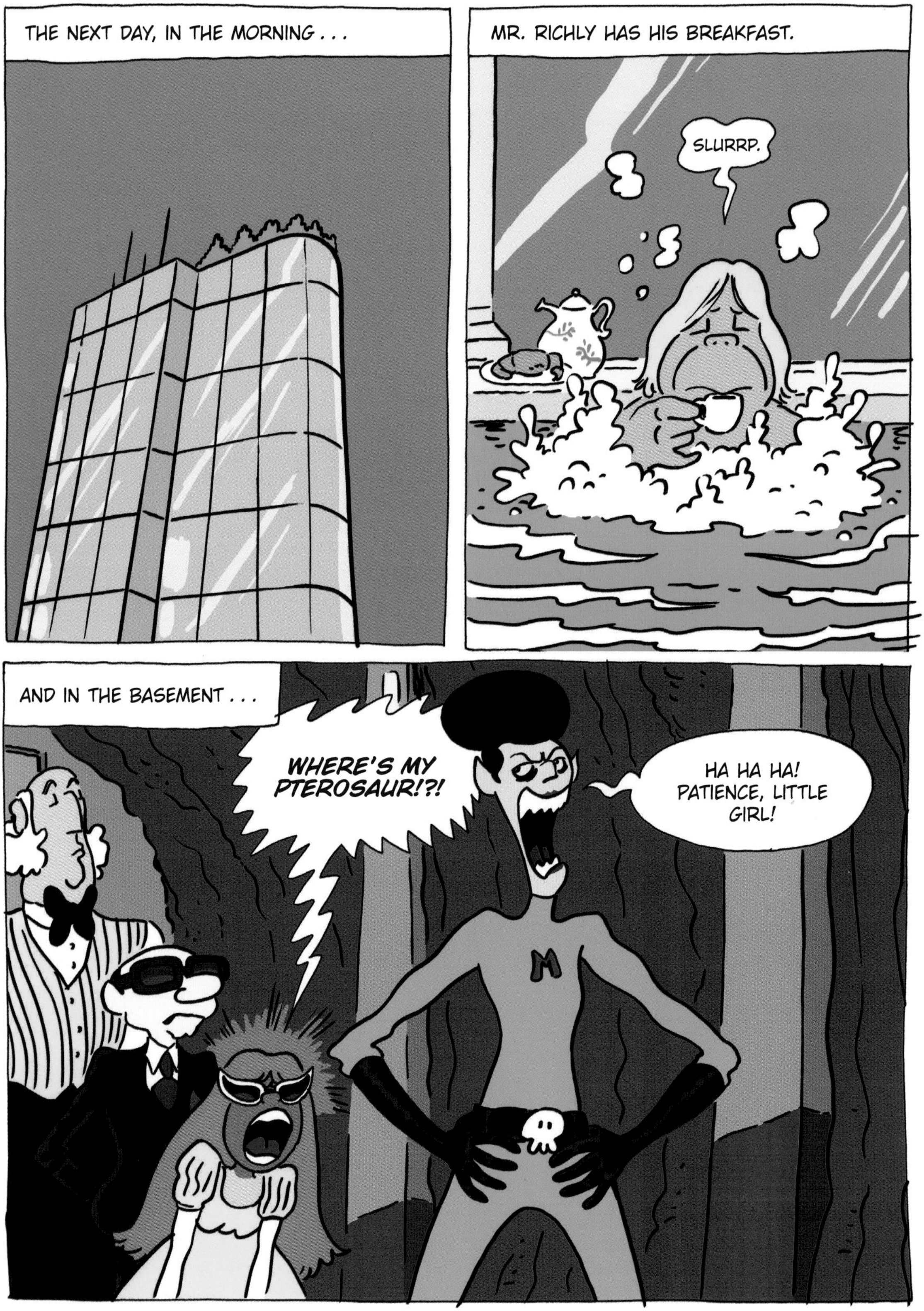
THE NEXT DAY, IN THE MORNING . . .
MR. RICHLY HAS HIS BREAKFAST.
SLURRP.
AND IN THE BASEMENT . . .
WHERE'S MY PTEROSAUR!?!
HA HA HA! PATIENCE, LITTLE GIRL!

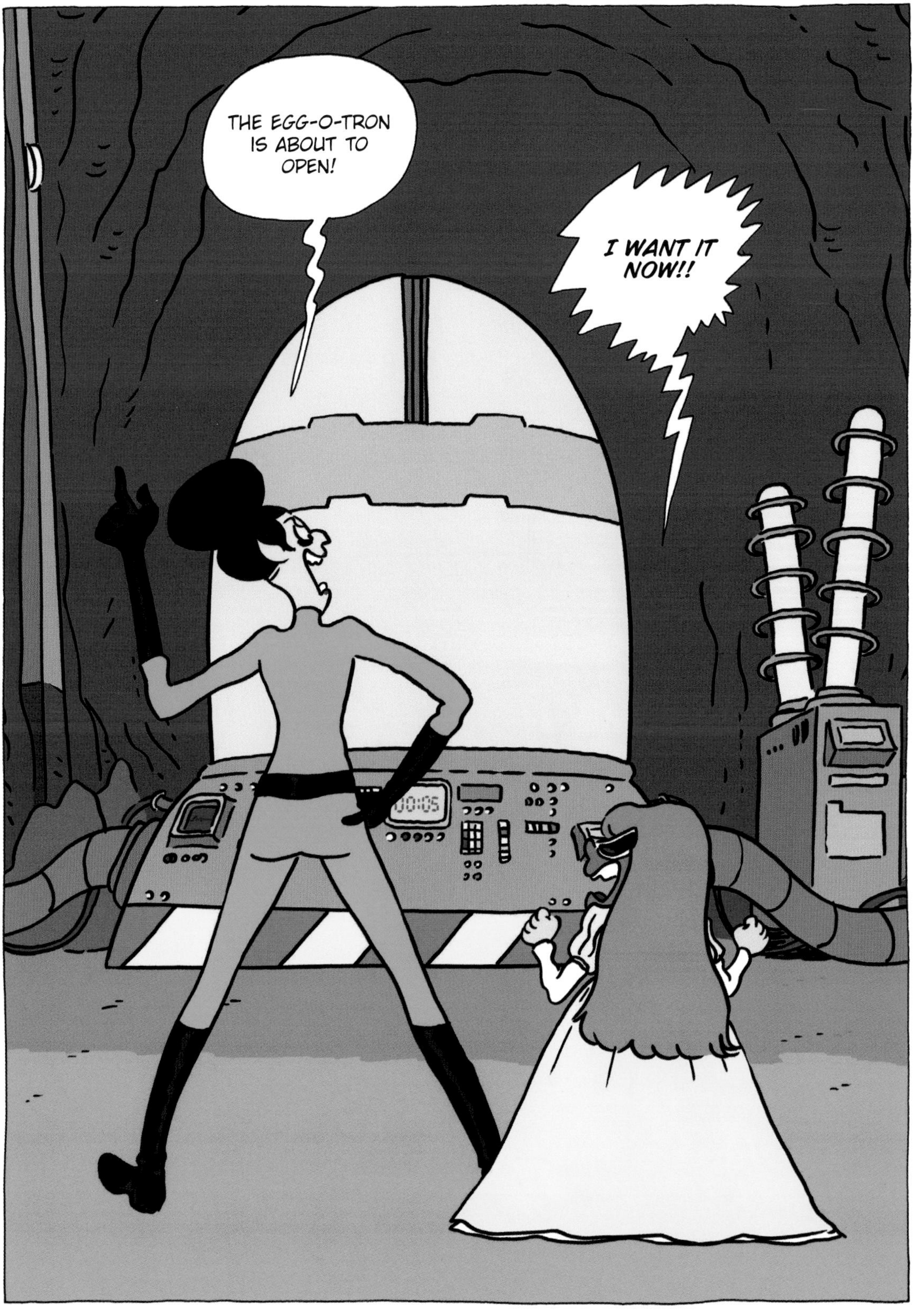
THE EGG-O-TRON IS ABOUT TO OPEN!
I WANT IT NOW!!
00:05

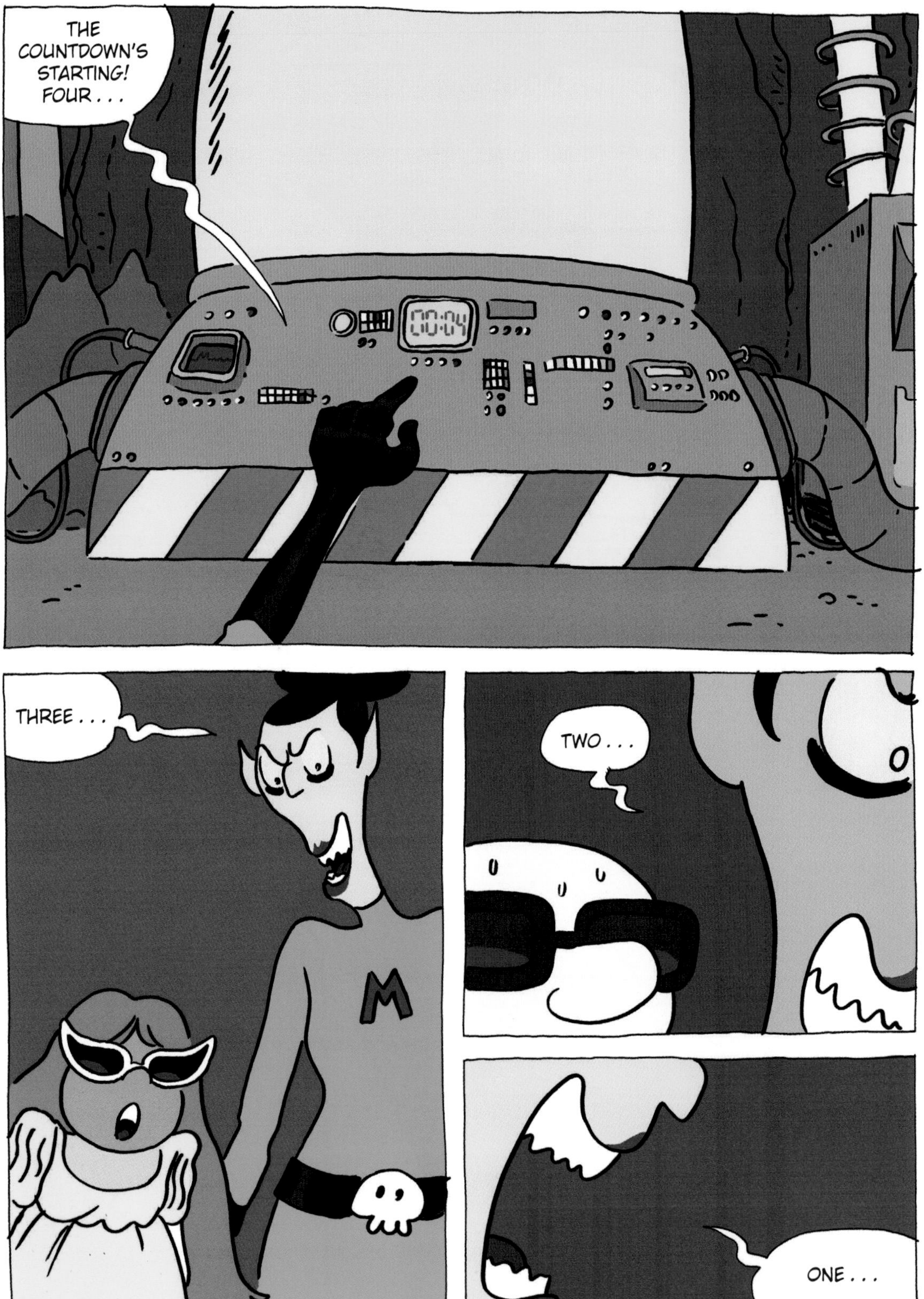
THE COUNTDOWN'S STARTING! FOUR . . .
00:04
THREE . . .
M
TWO . . .
ONE . . .

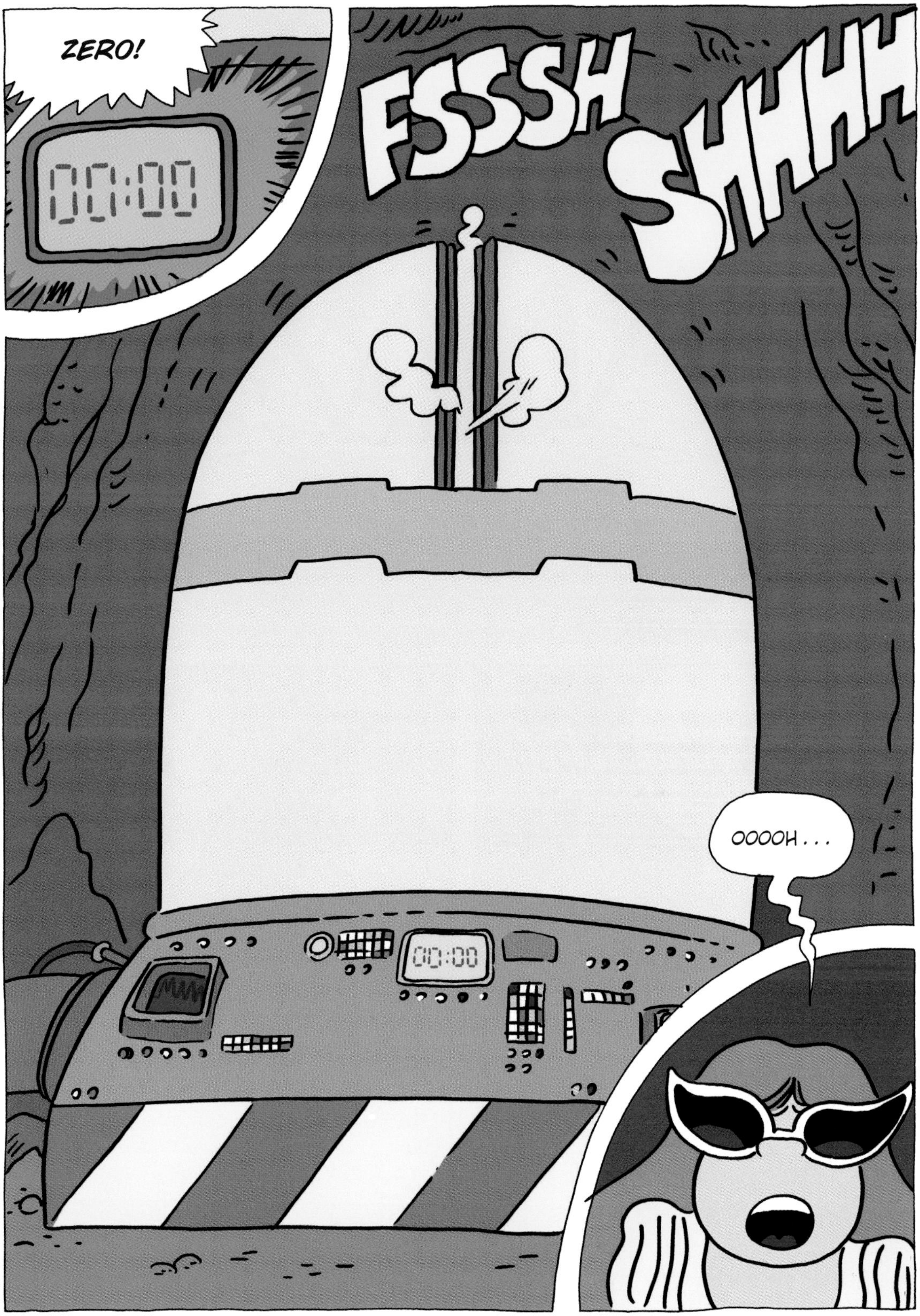
ZERO!
00:00
FSSSH
SHHHH
00:00
OOOOH...

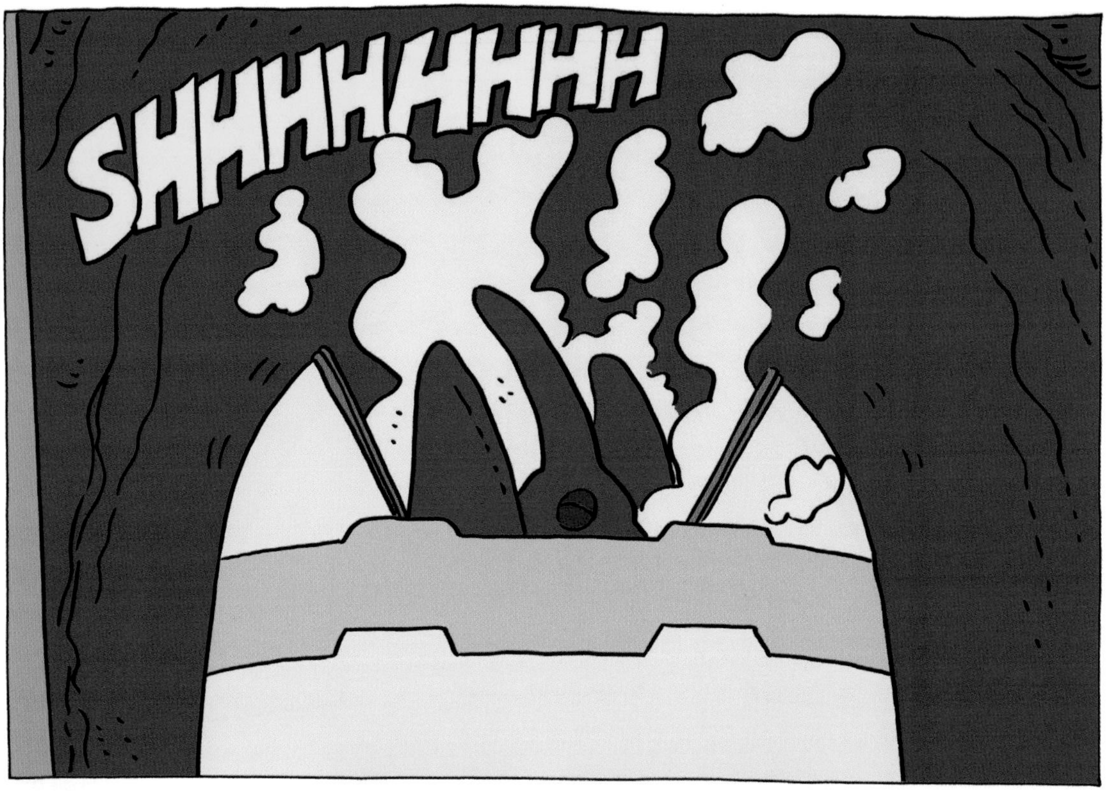
SHHHHHHHH

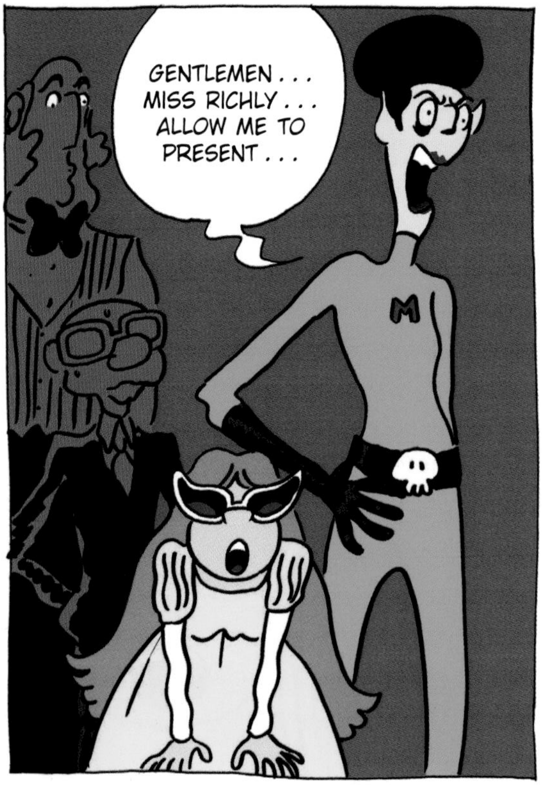
GENTLEMEN . . . MISS RICHLY . . . ALLOW ME TO PRESENT . . .

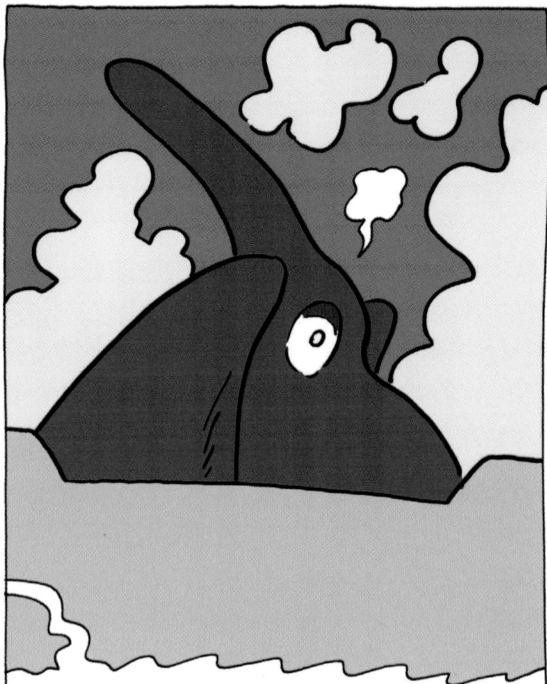
. . . AN AUTHENTIC PREHISTORIC PTEROSAUR.

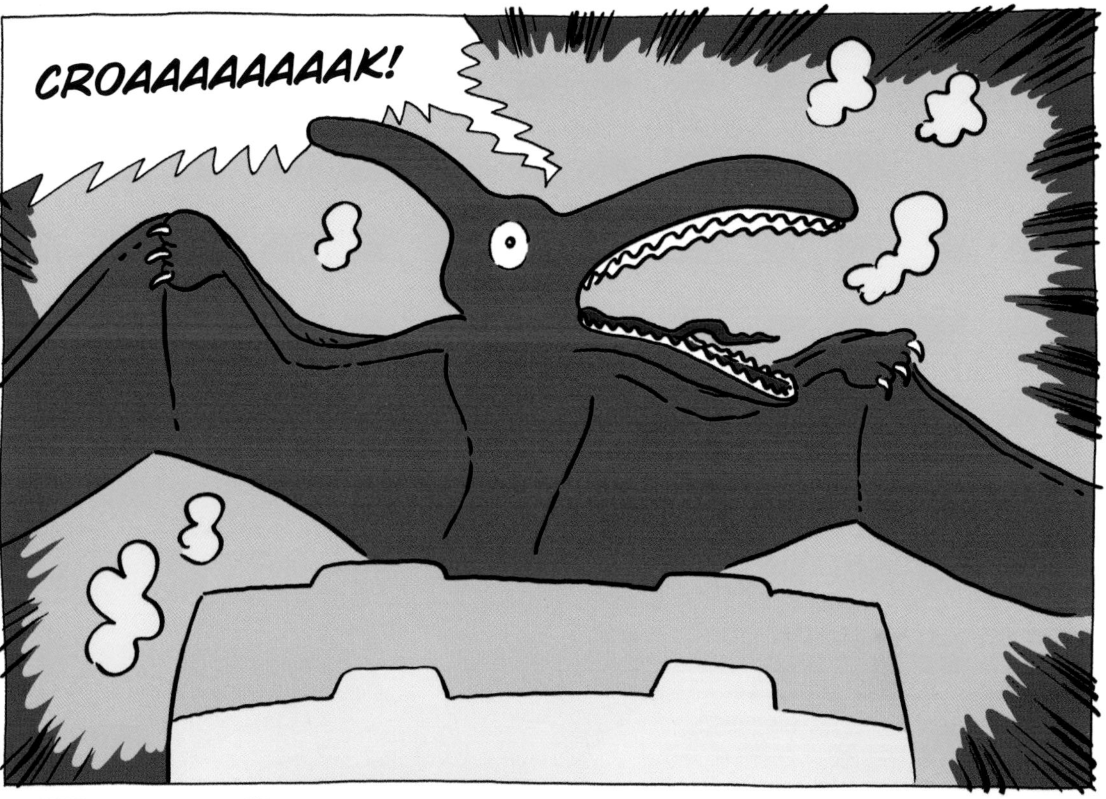
CROAAAAAAAAK!

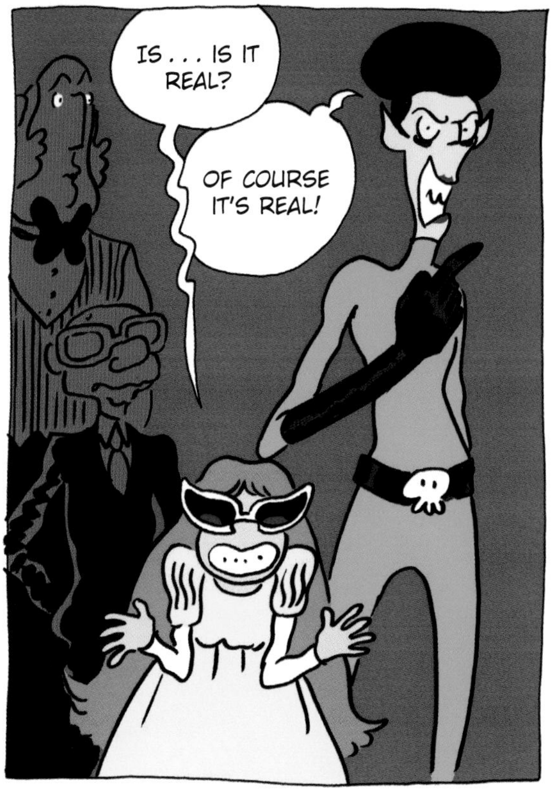
IS . . . IS IT REAL?
OF COURSE IT'S REAL!

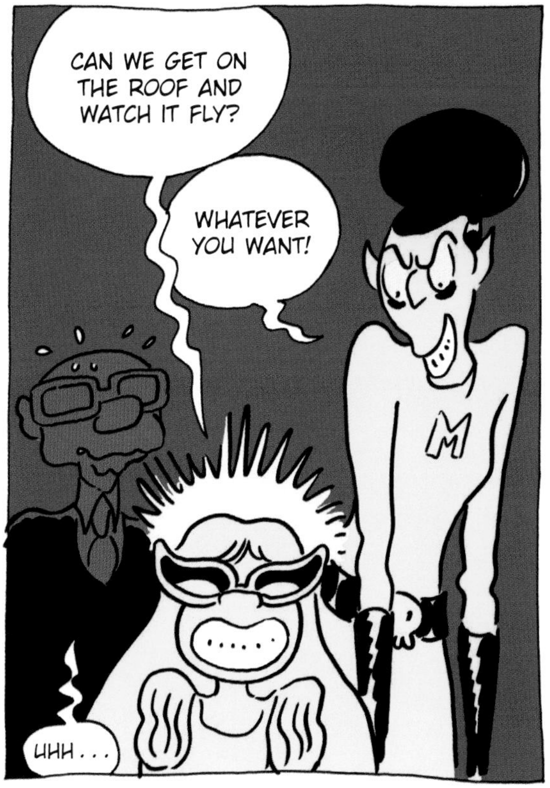
CAN WE GET ON THE ROOF AND WATCH IT FLY?
WHATEVER YOU WANT!
UHH . . .

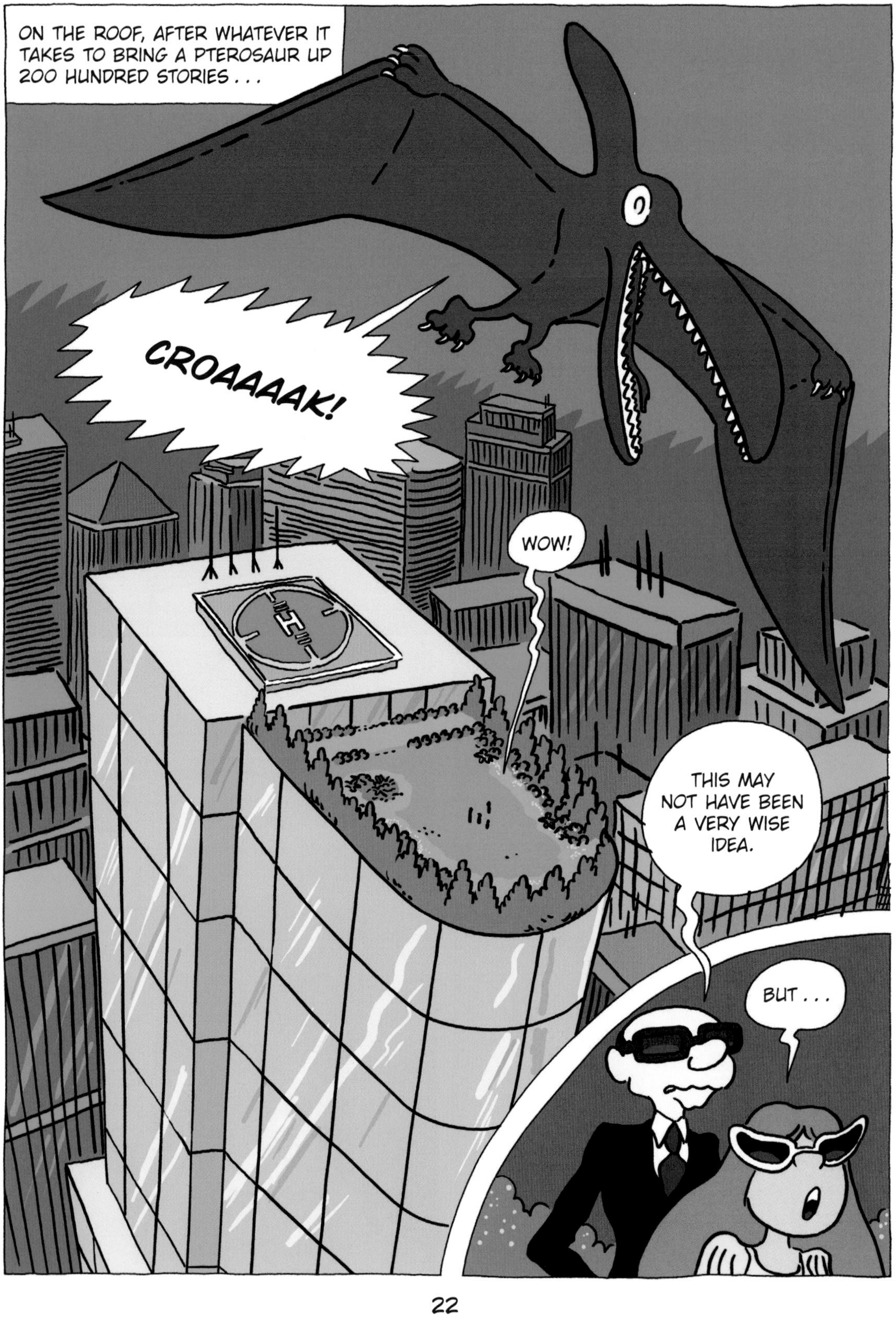
ON THE ROOF, AFTER WHATEVER IT TAKES TO BRING A PTEROSAUR UP 200 HUNDRED STORIES . . .
CROAAAAK!
WOW!
THIS MAY NOT HAVE BEEN A VERY WISE IDEA.
BUT . . .

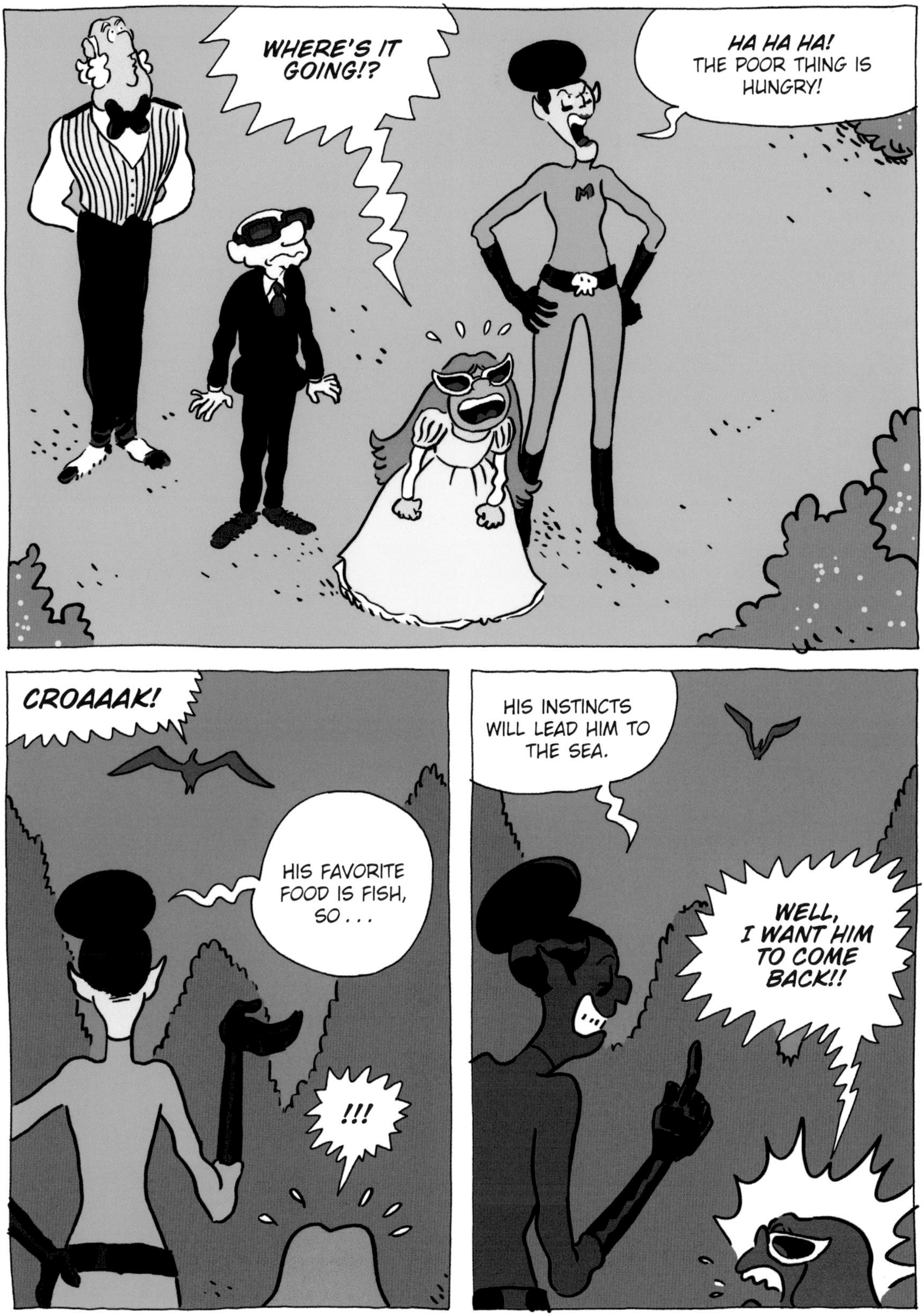
WHERE'S IT GOING!?
HA HA HA! THE POOR THING IS HUNGRY!
CROAAAK!
HIS FAVORITE FOOD IS FISH, SO . . .
!!!
HIS INSTINCTS WILL LEAD HIM TO THE SEA.
WELL, I WANT HIM TO COME BACK!!

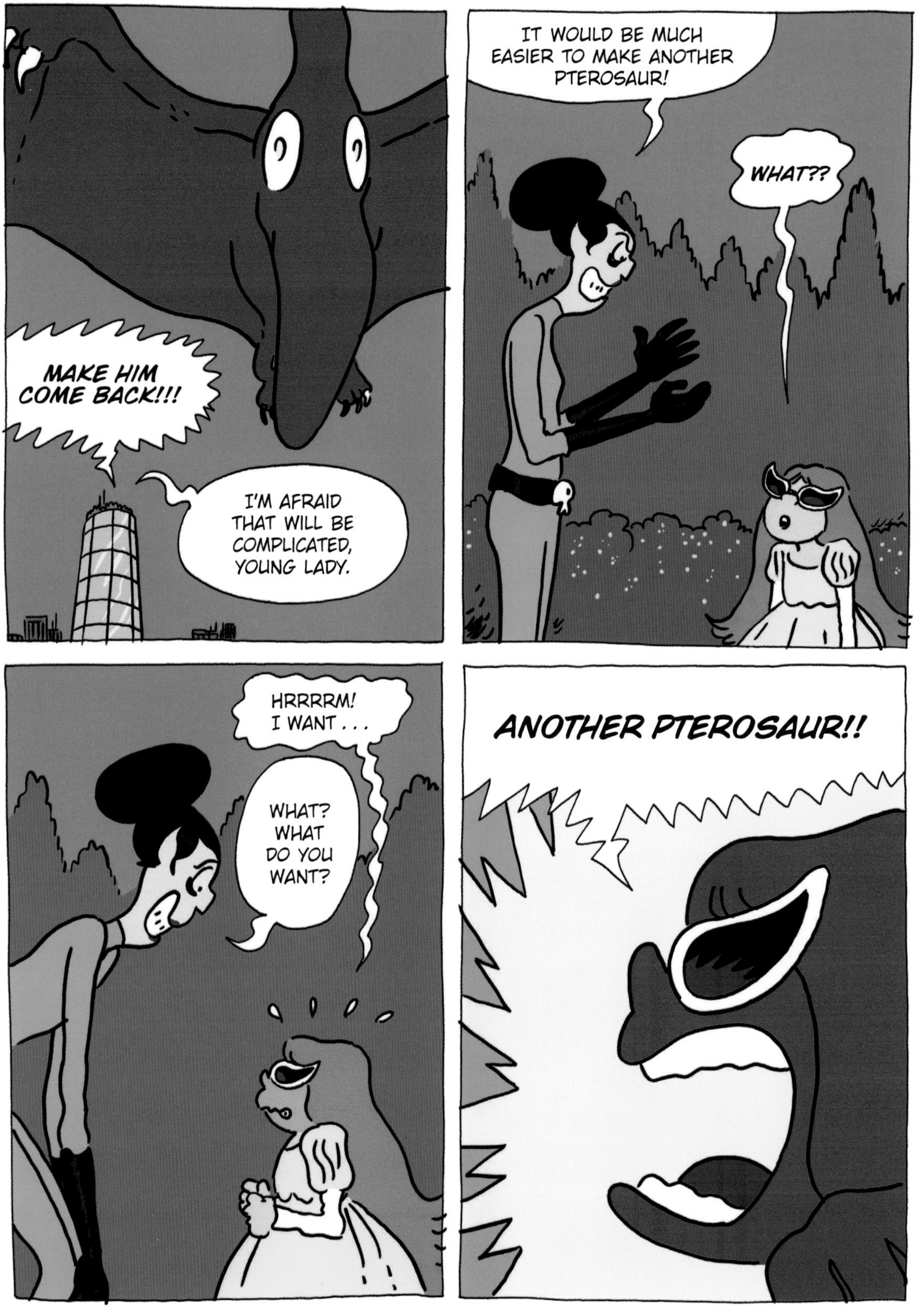
MAKE HIM COME BACK!!!
I'M AFRAID THAT WILL BE COMPLICATED, YOUNG LADY.
IT WOULD BE MUCH EASIER TO MAKE ANOTHER PTEROSAUR!
WHAT??
HRRRRM! I WANT . . .
WHAT? WHAT DO YOU WANT?
ANOTHER PTEROSAUR!!

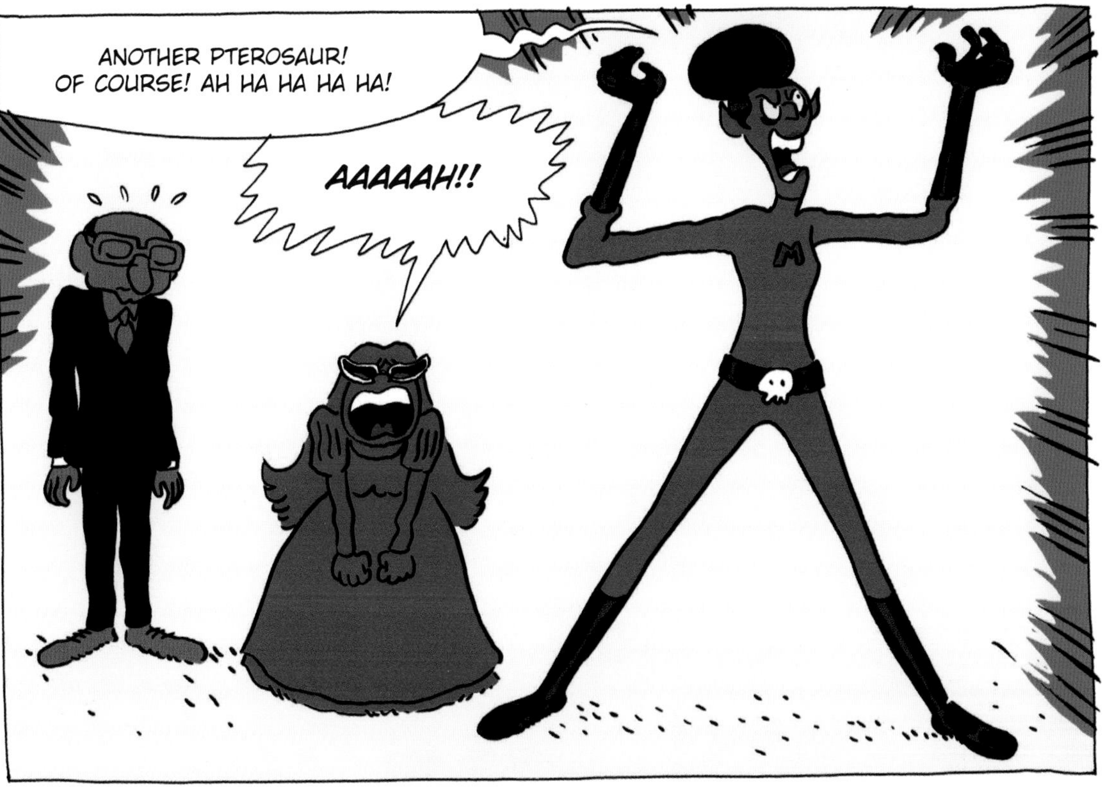
ANOTHER PTEROSAUR! OF COURSE! AH HA HA HA HA!
AAAAAH!!

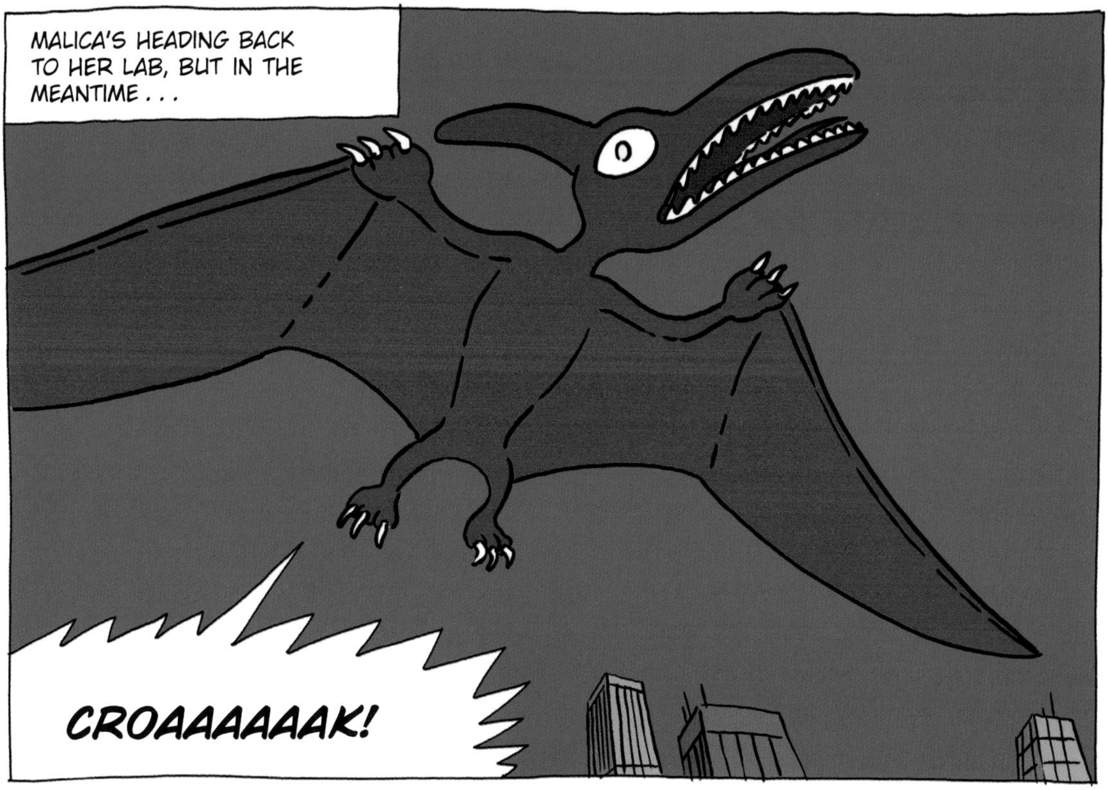
MALICA'S HEADING BACK TO HER LAB, BUT IN THE MEANTIME . . .
CROAAAAAAK!

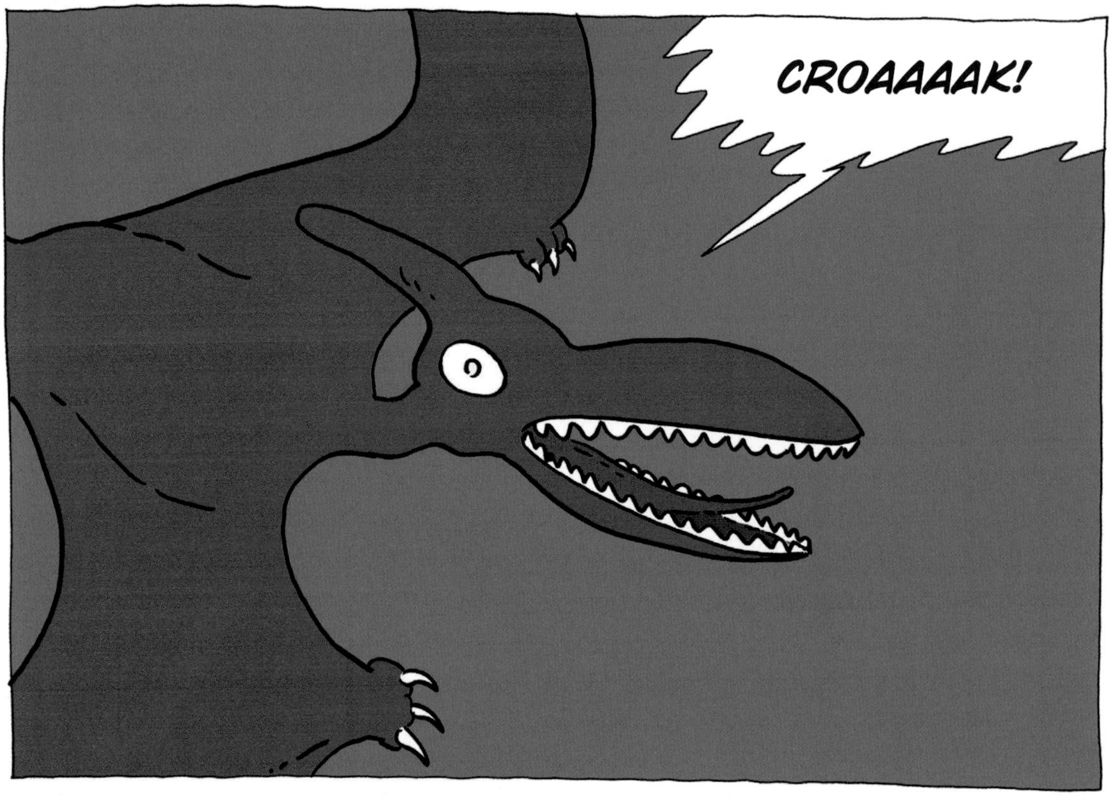
CROAAAAK!

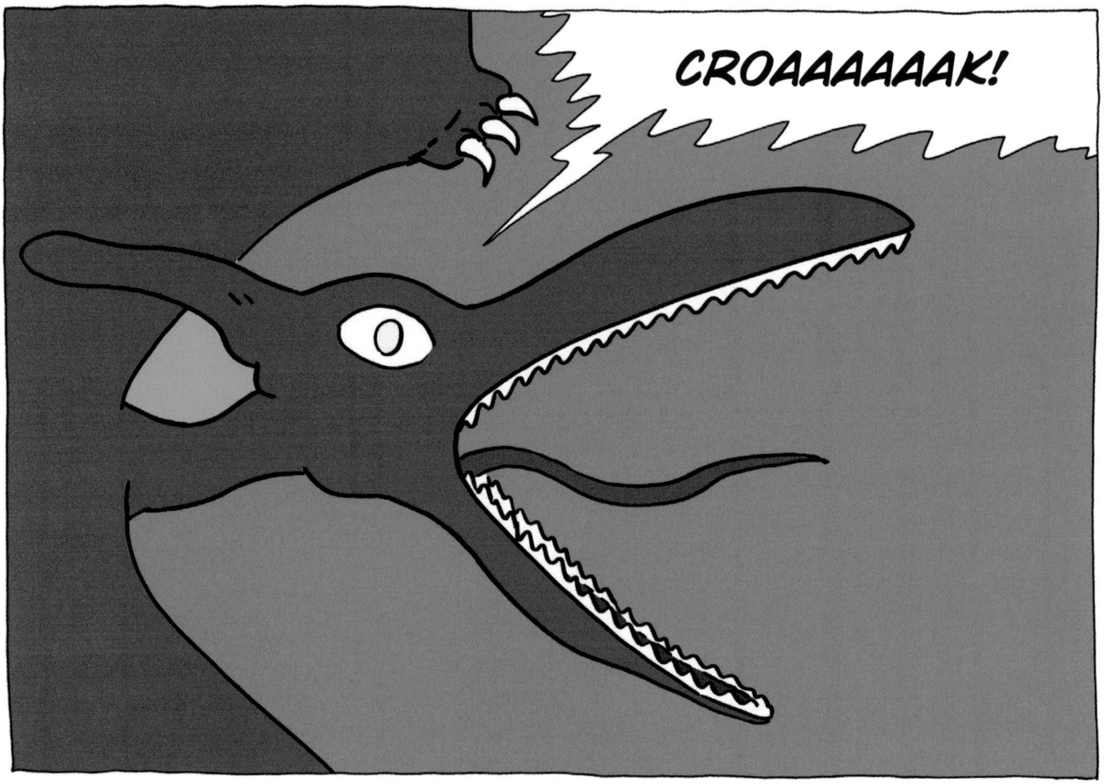
CROAAAAAAK!

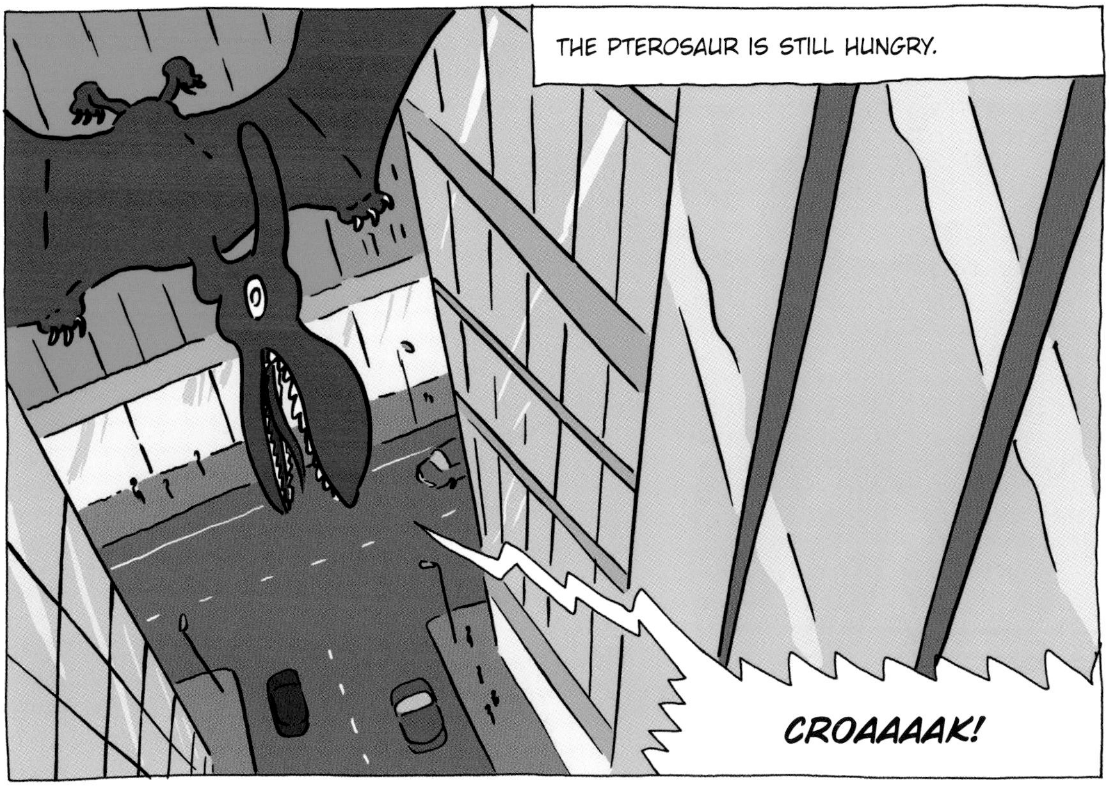
THE PTEROSAUR IS STILL HUNGRY.
CROAAAAK!

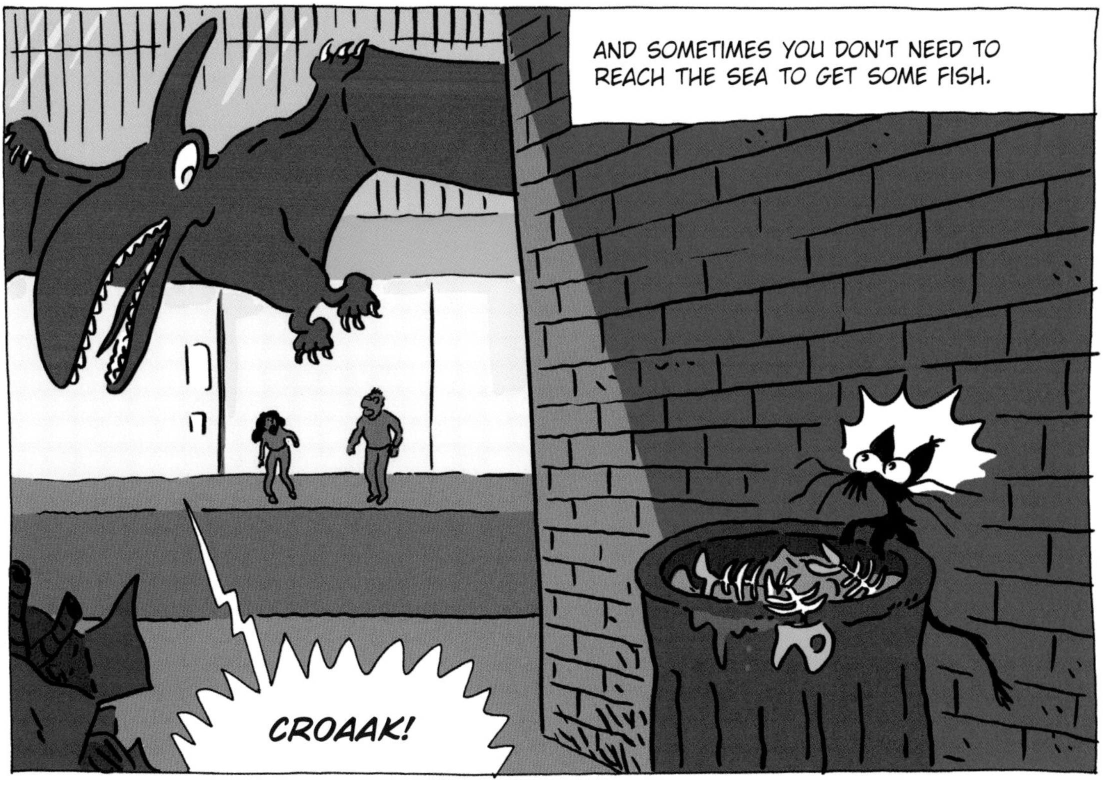
AND SOMETIMES YOU DON'T NEED TO REACH THE SEA TO GET SOME FISH.
CROAAK!

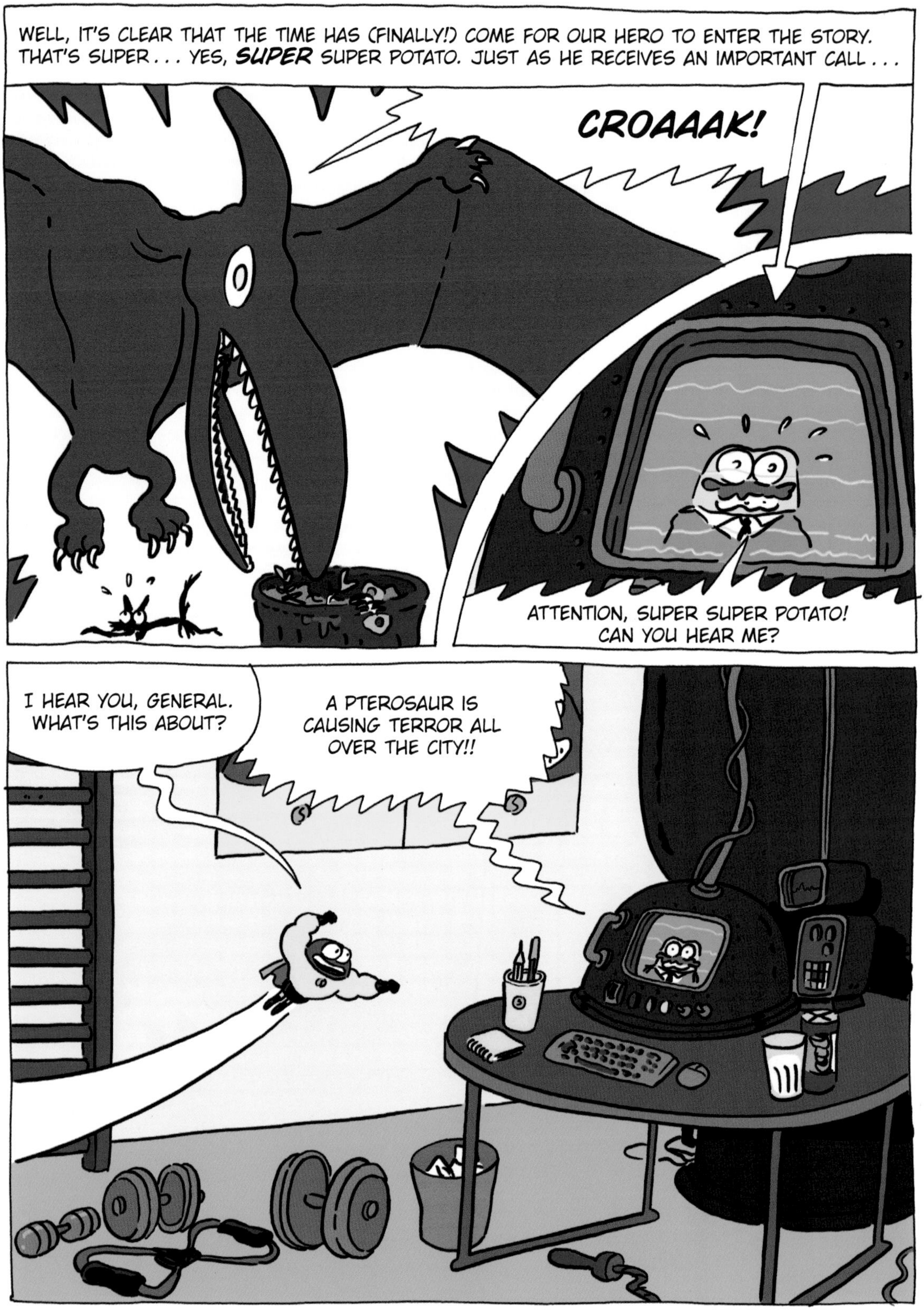
WELL, IT'S CLEAR THAT THE TIME HAS (FINALLY!) COME FOR OUR HERO TO ENTER THE STORY. THAT'S SUPER . . . YES, **SUPER** SUPER POTATO. JUST AS HE RECEIVES AN IMPORTANT CALL . . .
CROAAAK!
ATTENTION, SUPER SUPER POTATO! CAN YOU HEAR ME?
I HEAR YOU, GENERAL. WHAT'S THIS ABOUT?
A PTEROSAUR IS CAUSING TERROR ALL OVER THE CITY!!

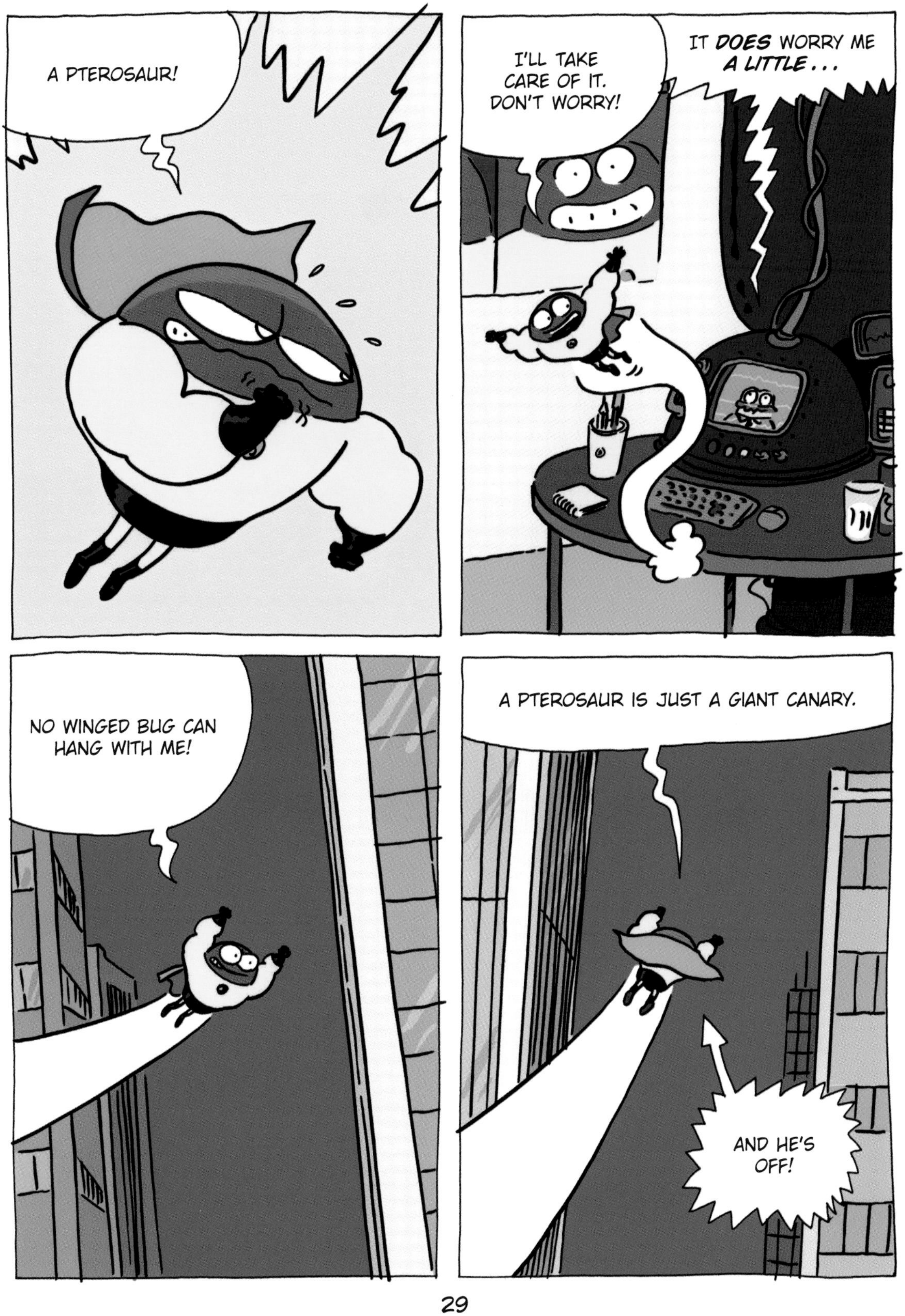
A PTEROSAUR!
I'LL TAKE CARE OF IT. DON'T WORRY!
IT DOES WORRY ME A LITTLE . . .
NO WINGED BUG CAN HANG WITH ME!
A PTEROSAUR IS JUST A GIANT CANARY.
AND HE'S OFF!

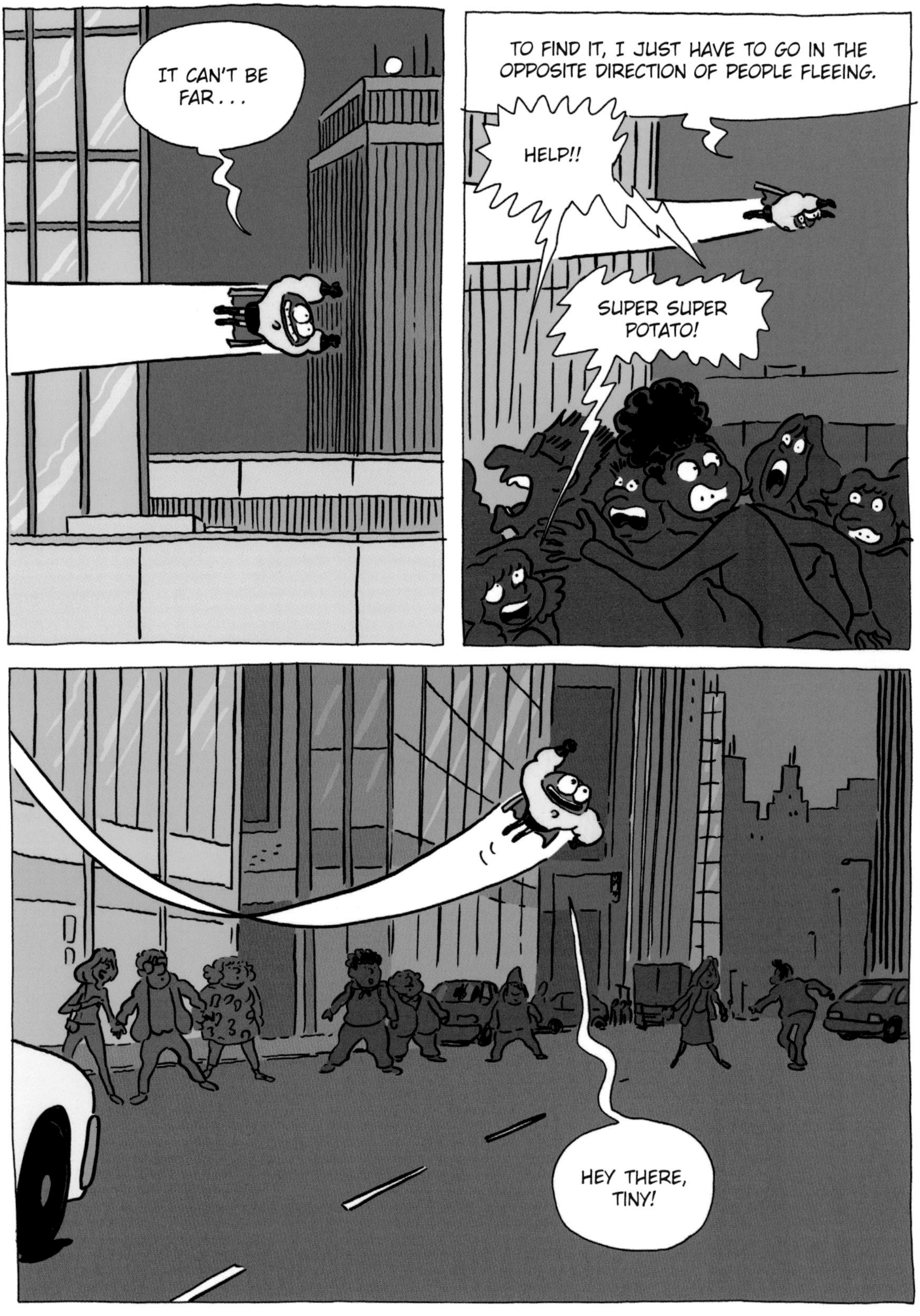
IT CAN'T BE FAR . . .
TO FIND IT, I JUST HAVE TO GO IN THE OPPOSITE DIRECTION OF PEOPLE FLEEING.
HELP!!
SUPER SUPER POTATO!
HEY THERE, TINY!

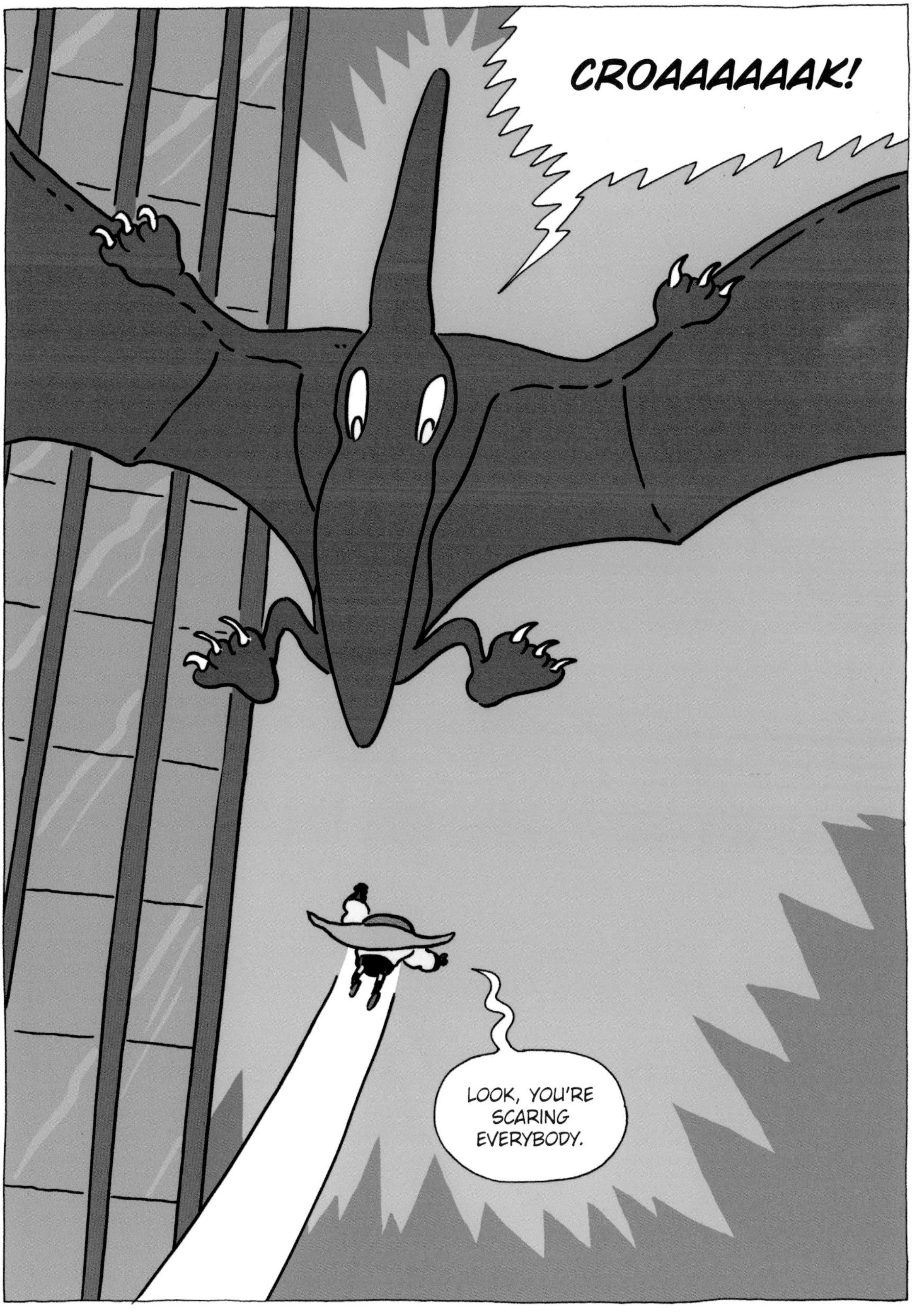
CROAAAAAAK!
LOOK, YOU'RE SCARING EVERYBODY.

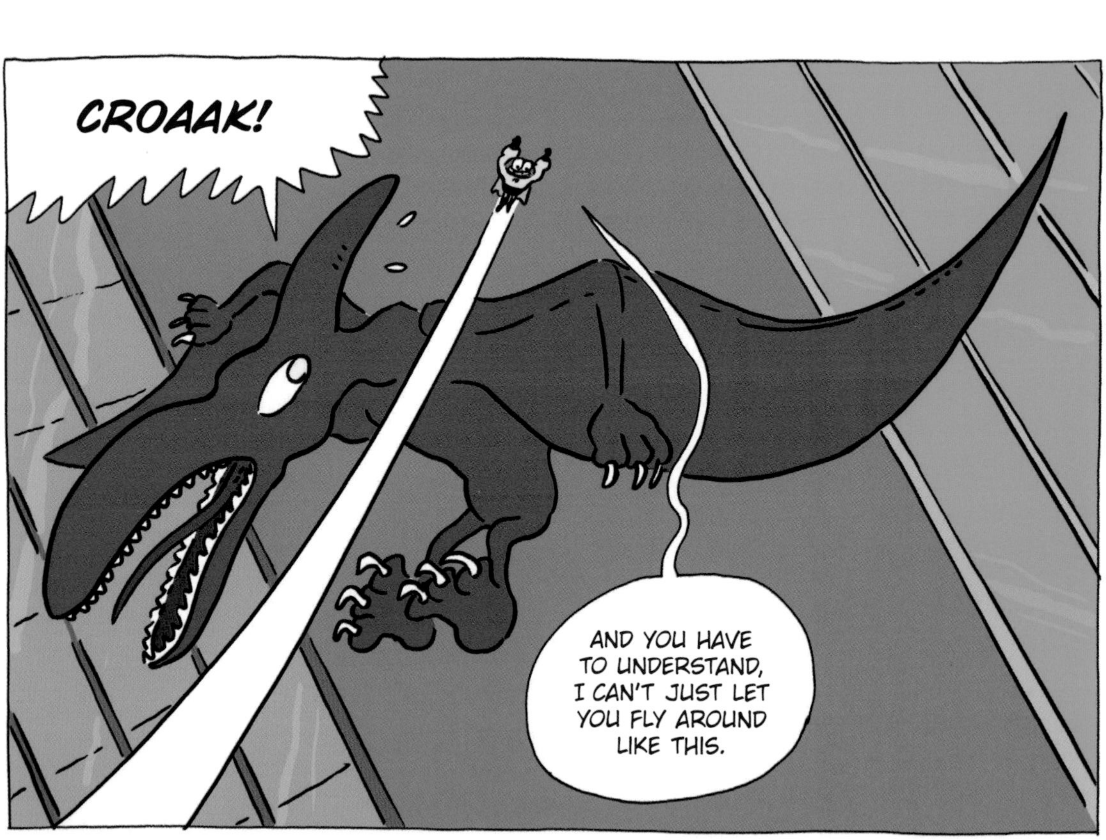
CROAAK!
AND YOU HAVE TO UNDERSTAND, I CAN'T JUST LET YOU FLY AROUND LIKE THIS.

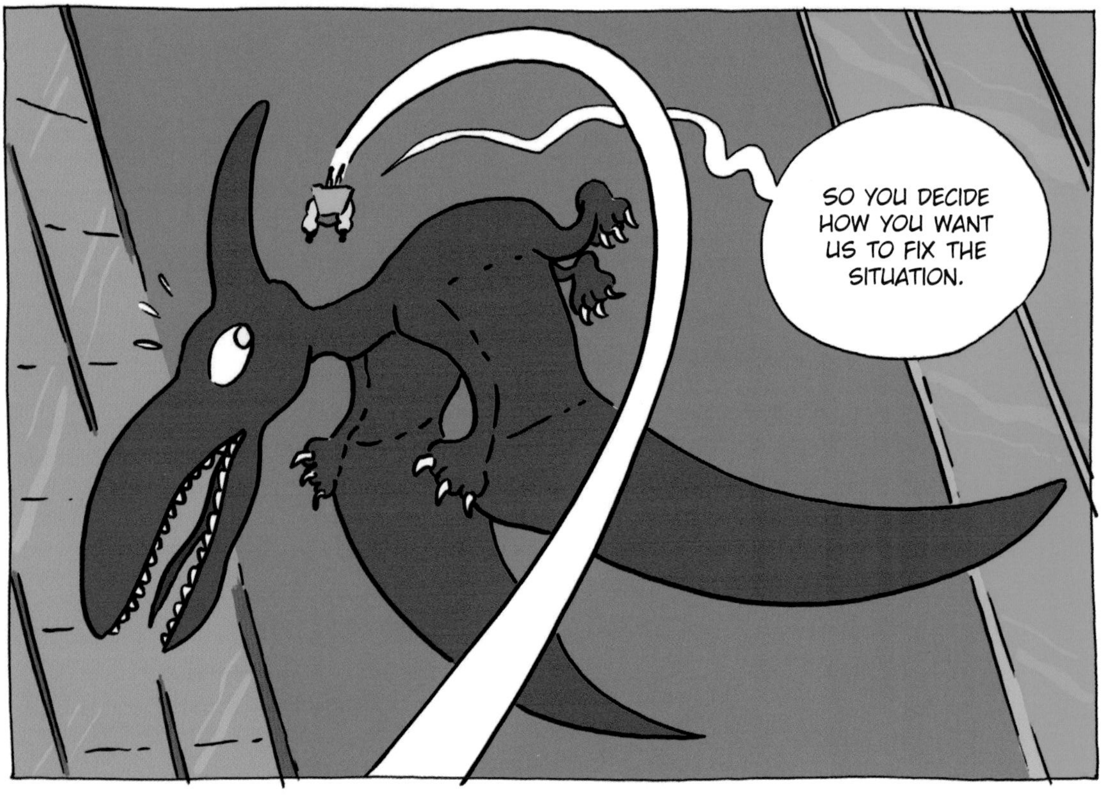
SO YOU DECIDE HOW YOU WANT US TO FIX THE SITUATION.

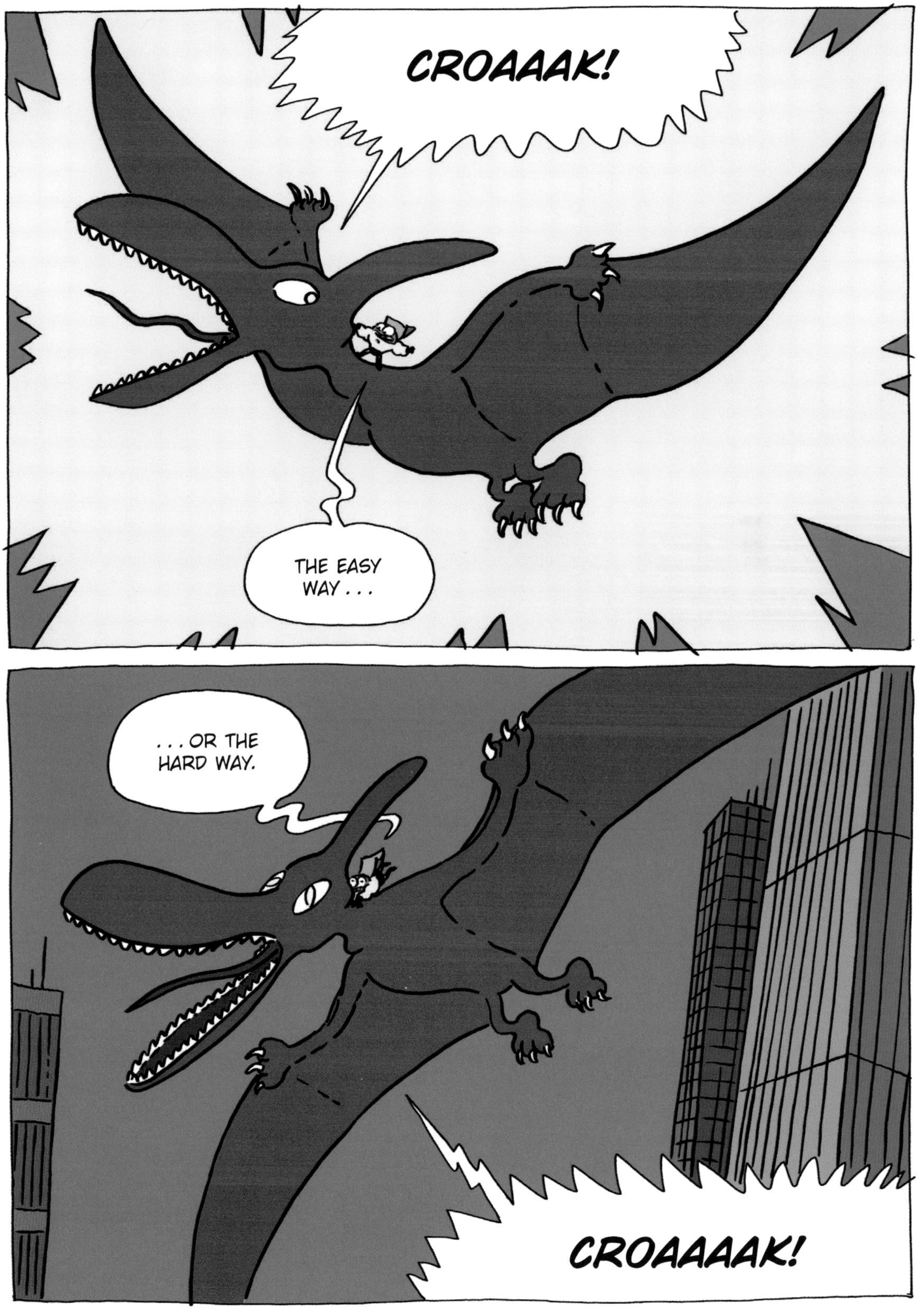
CROAAAK!
THE EASY WAY . . .
. . . OR THE HARD WAY.
CROAAAAK!

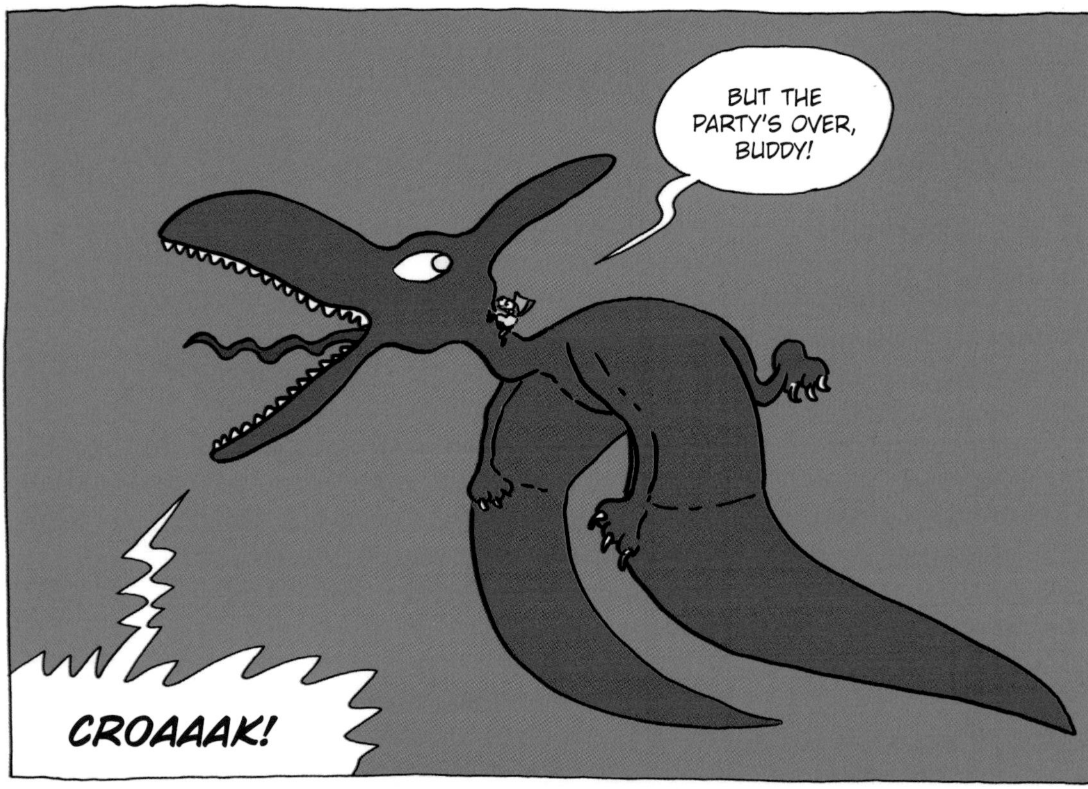
BUT THE PARTY'S OVER, BUDDY!
CROAAAK!

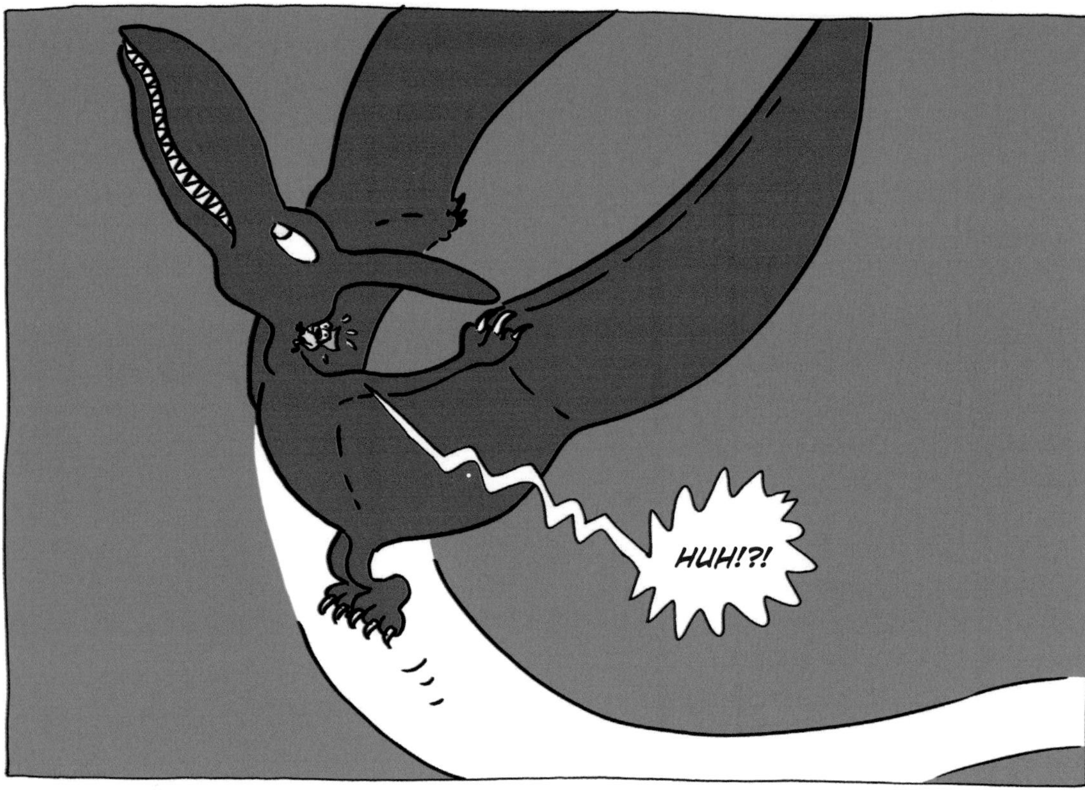
HUH!?!

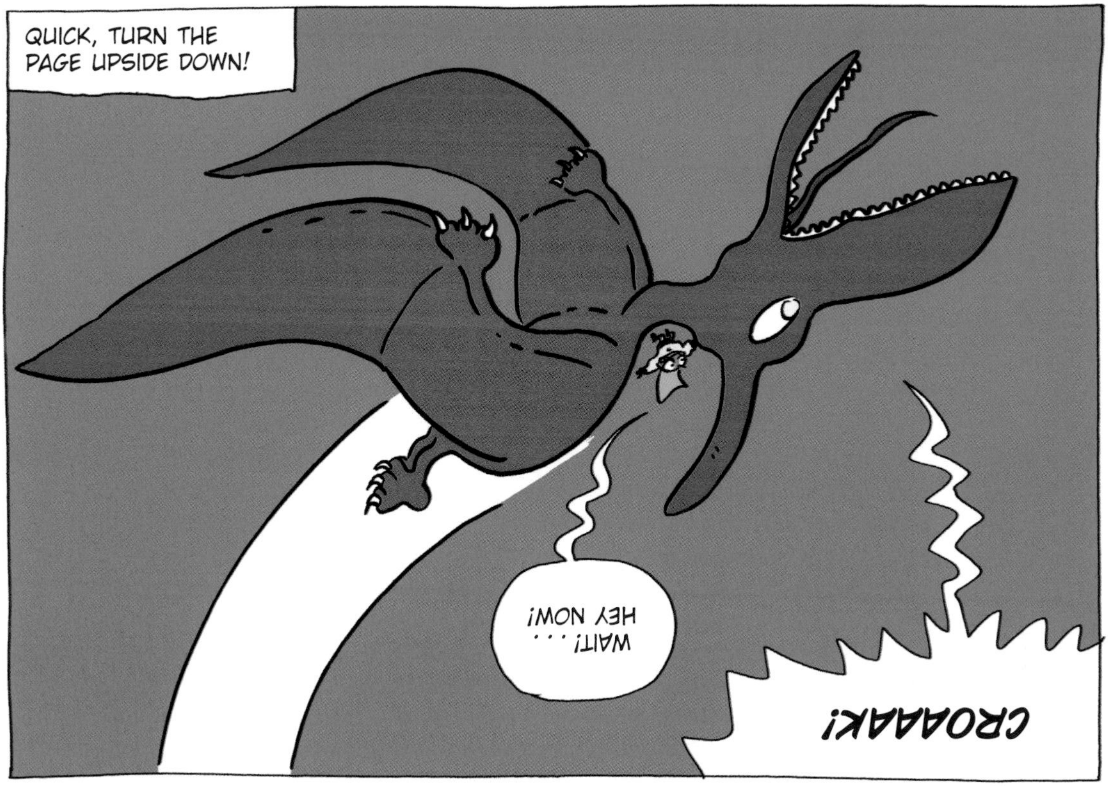
QUICK, TURN THE PAGE UPSIDE DOWN!
WAIT! . . . HEY NOW!
CROAAAK!

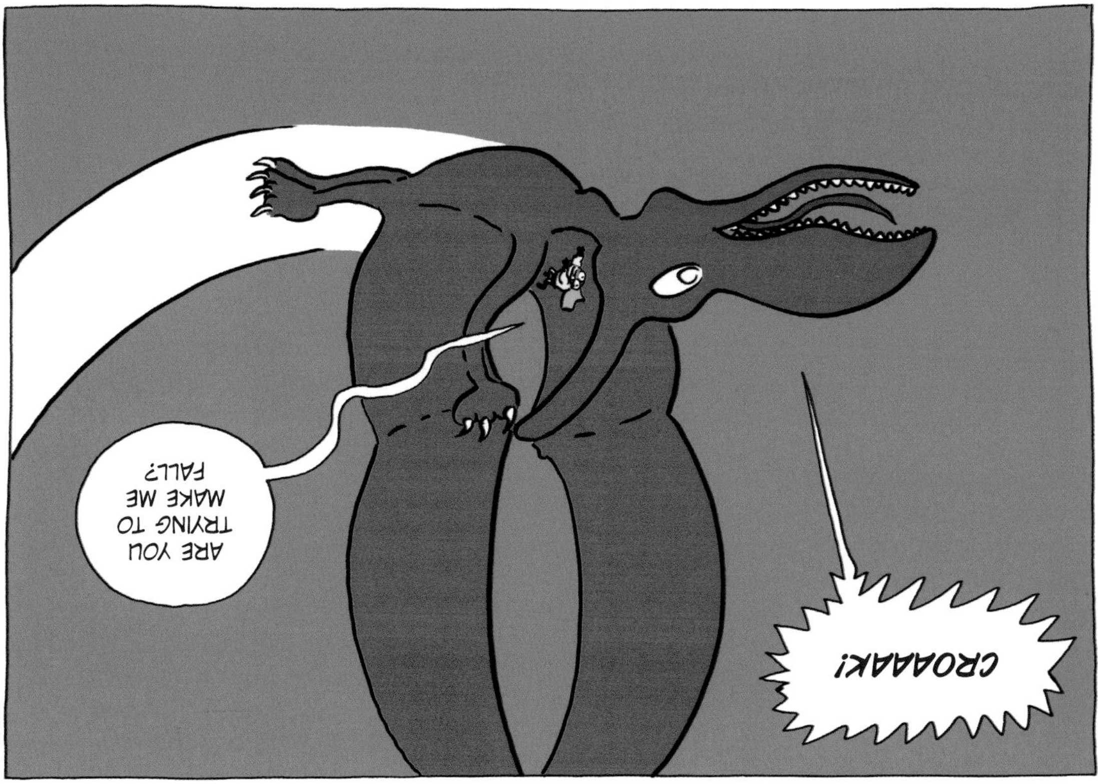
ARE YOU TRYING TO MAKE ME FALL?
CROAAAK!

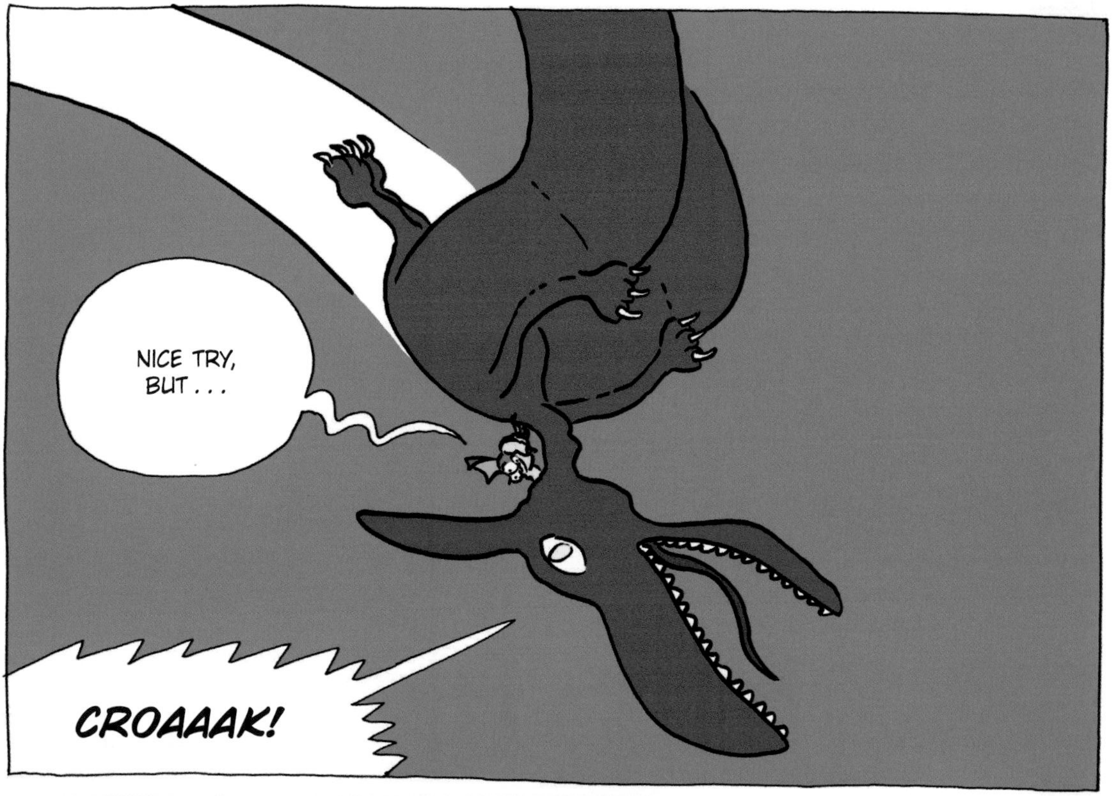
NICE TRY, BUT . . .
CROAAAK!

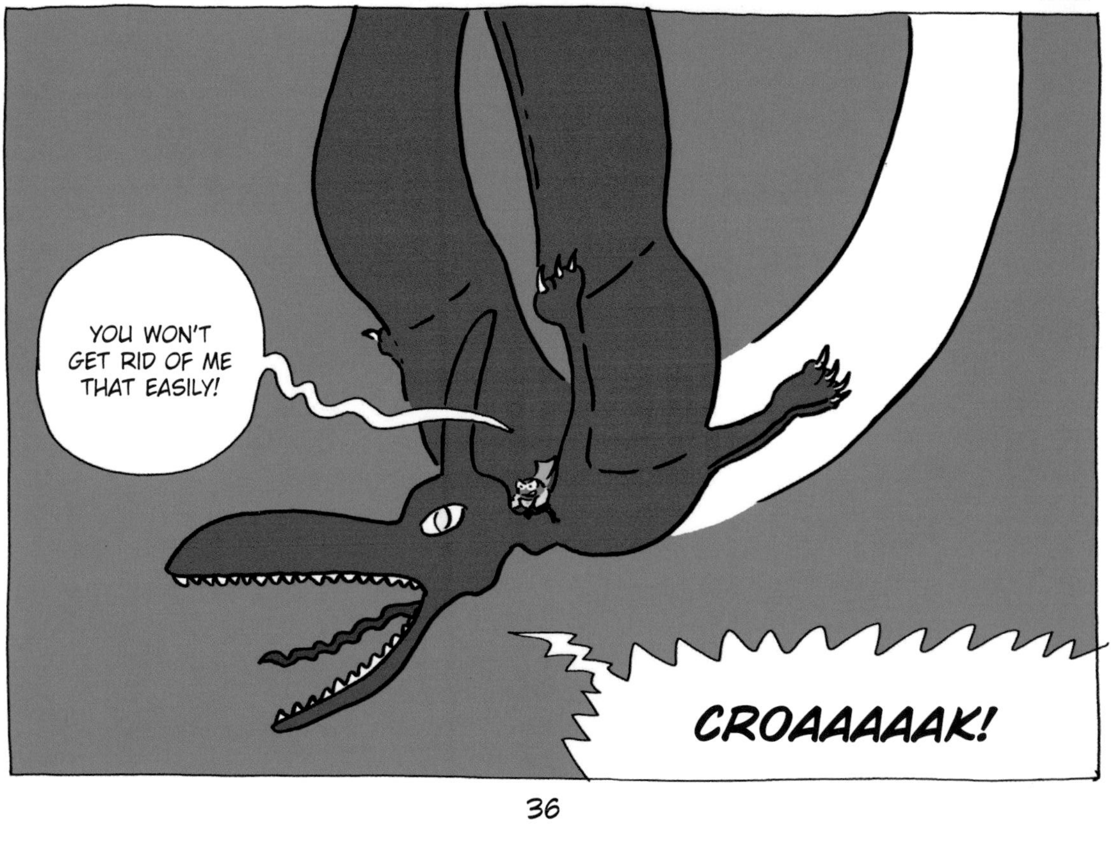
YOU WON'T GET RID OF ME THAT EASILY!
CROAAAAAK!

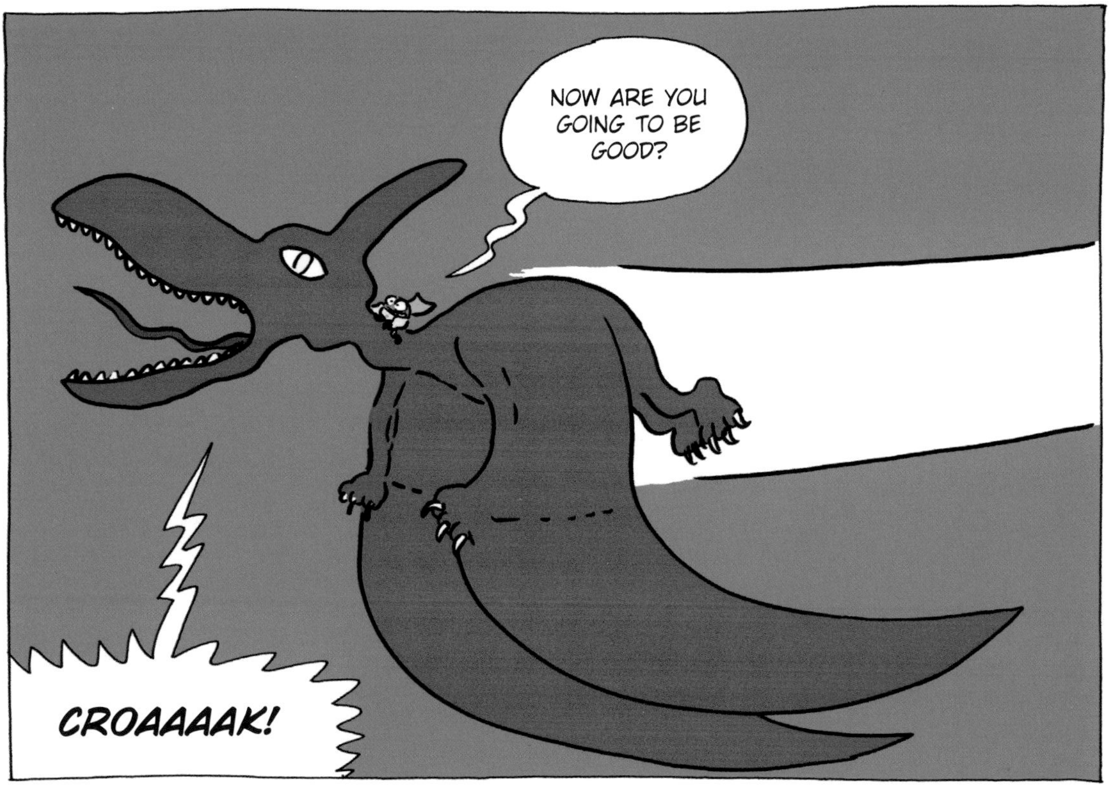
NOW ARE YOU GOING TO BE GOOD?
CROAAAAK!

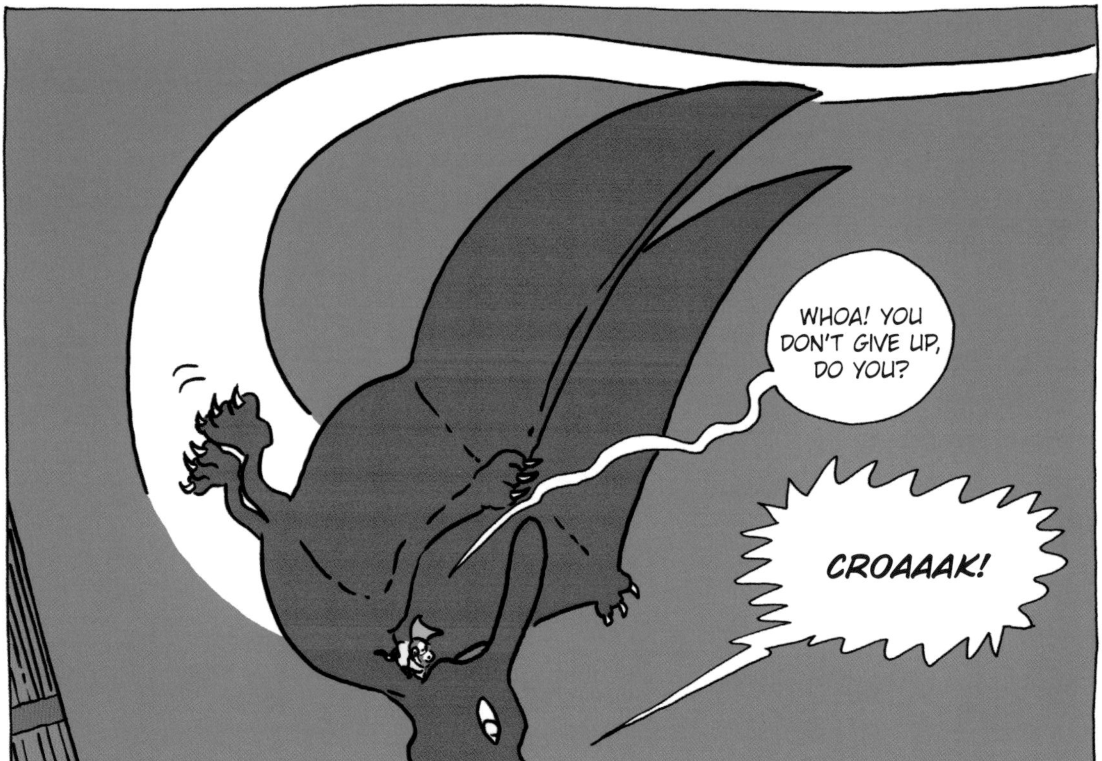
WHOA! YOU DON'T GIVE UP, DO YOU?
CROAAAK!

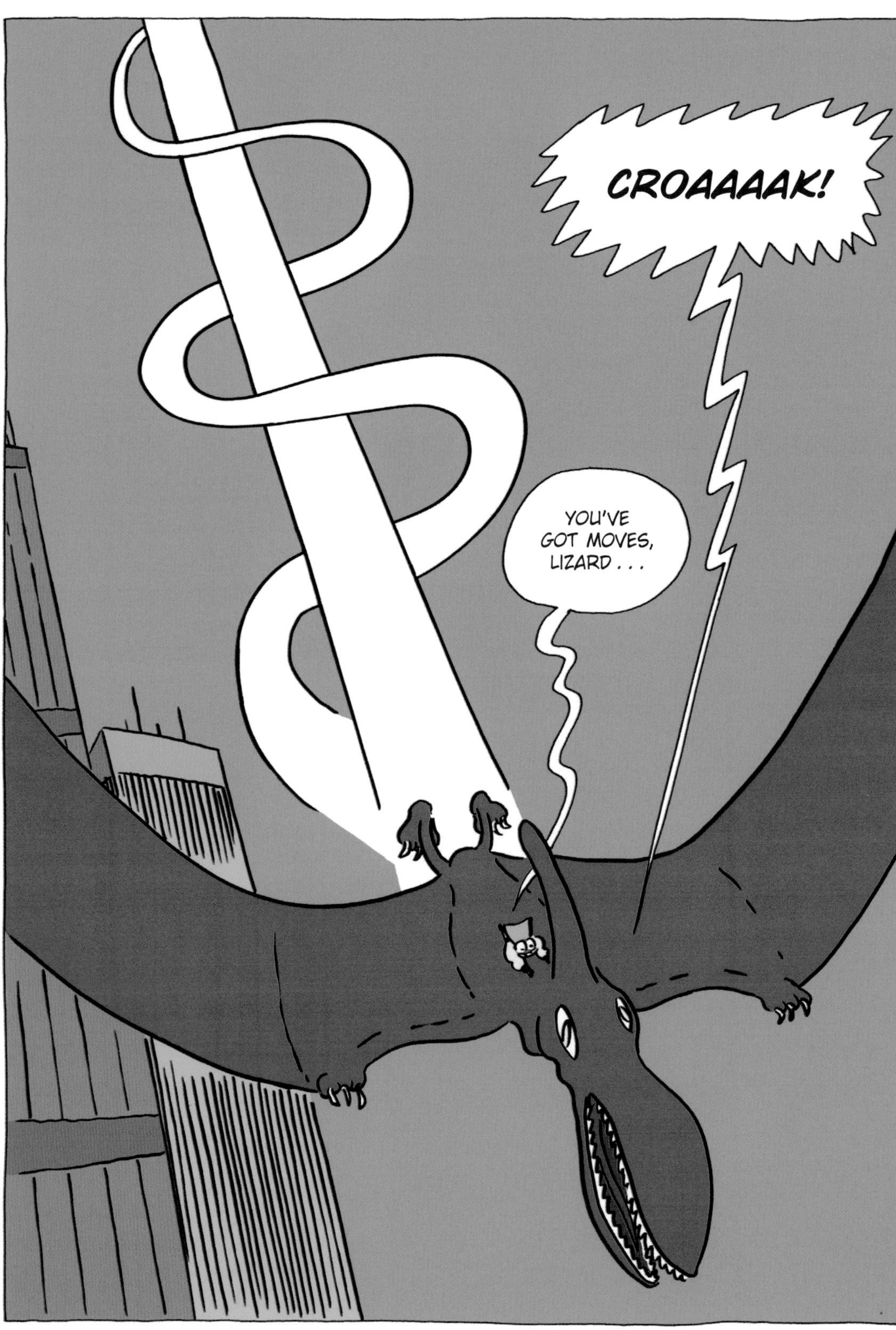
CROAAAAK!
YOU'VE GOT MOVES, LIZARD . . .

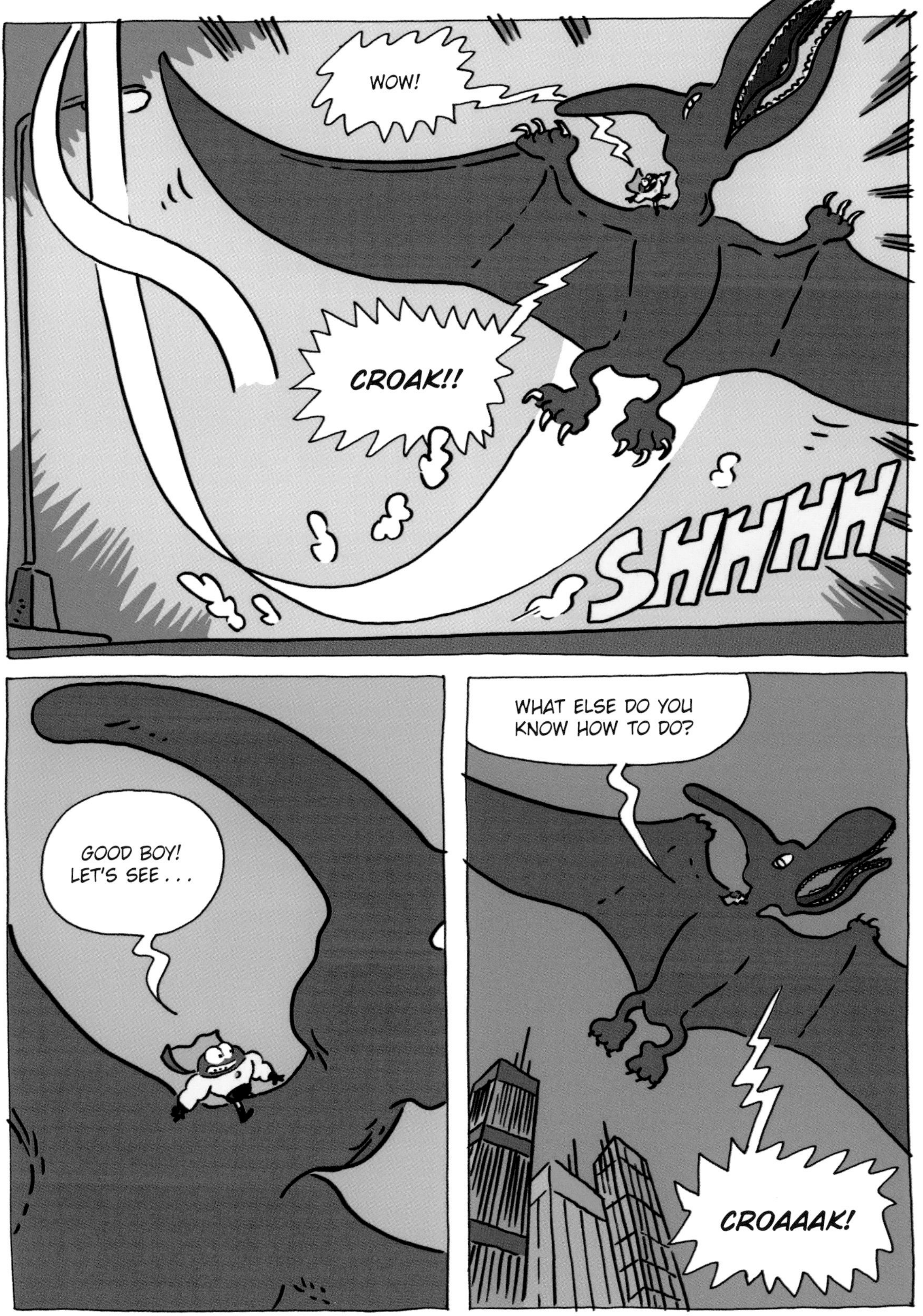
WOW!
CROAK!!
SHHHH
GOOD BOY! LET'S SEE . . .
WHAT ELSE DO YOU KNOW HOW TO DO?
CROAAAK!

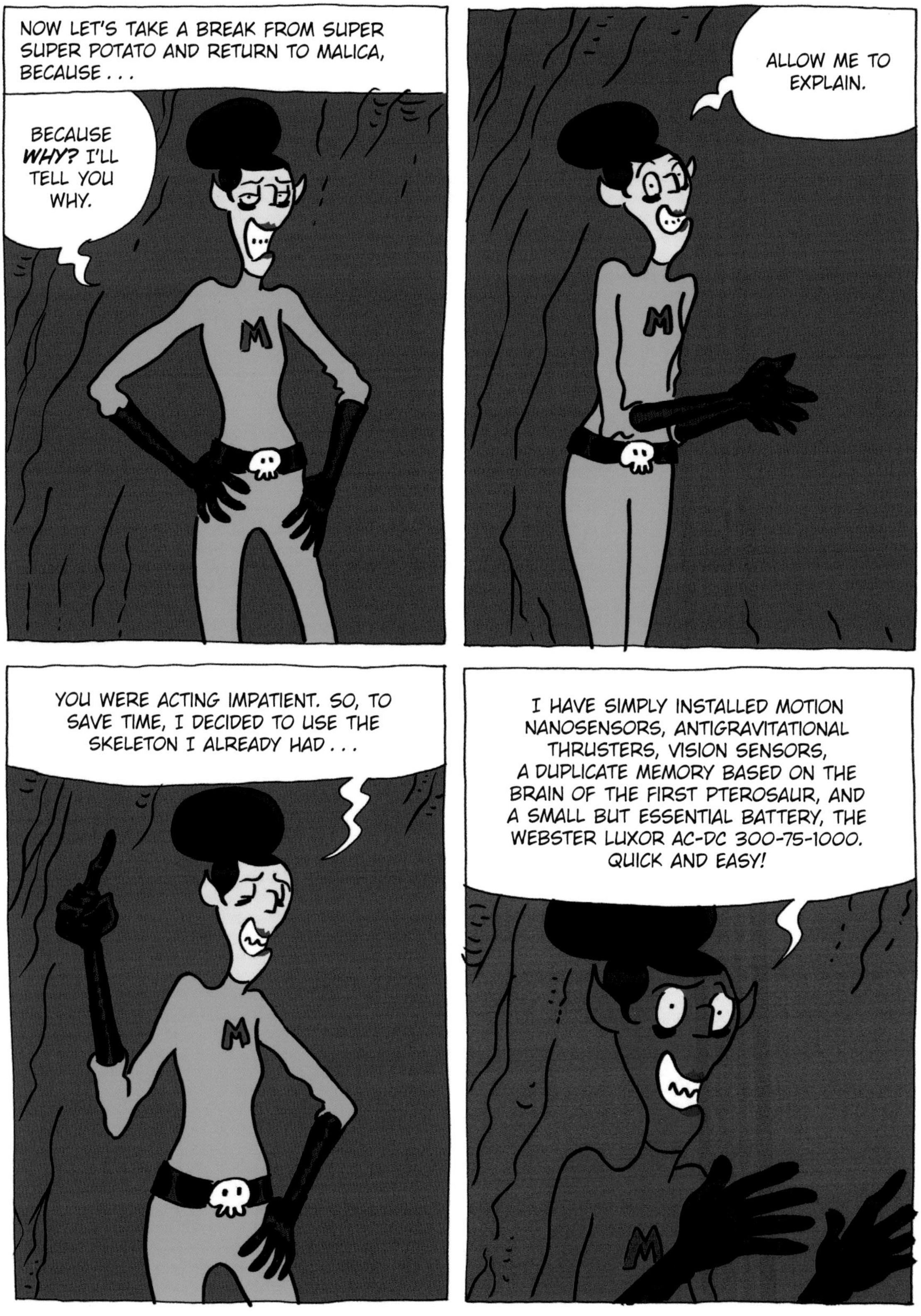
NOW LET'S TAKE A BREAK FROM SUPER SUPER POTATO AND RETURN TO MALICA, BECAUSE . . .
BECAUSE ***WHY?*** I'LL TELL YOU WHY.
ALLOW ME TO EXPLAIN.
YOU WERE ACTING IMPATIENT. SO, TO SAVE TIME, I DECIDED TO USE THE SKELETON I ALREADY HAD . . .
I HAVE SIMPLY INSTALLED MOTION NANOSENSORS, ANTIGRAVITATIONAL THRUSTERS, VISION SENSORS, A DUPLICATE MEMORY BASED ON THE BRAIN OF THE FIRST PTEROSAUR, AND A SMALL BUT ESSENTIAL BATTERY, THE WEBSTER LUXOR AC-DC 300-75-1000. QUICK AND EASY!

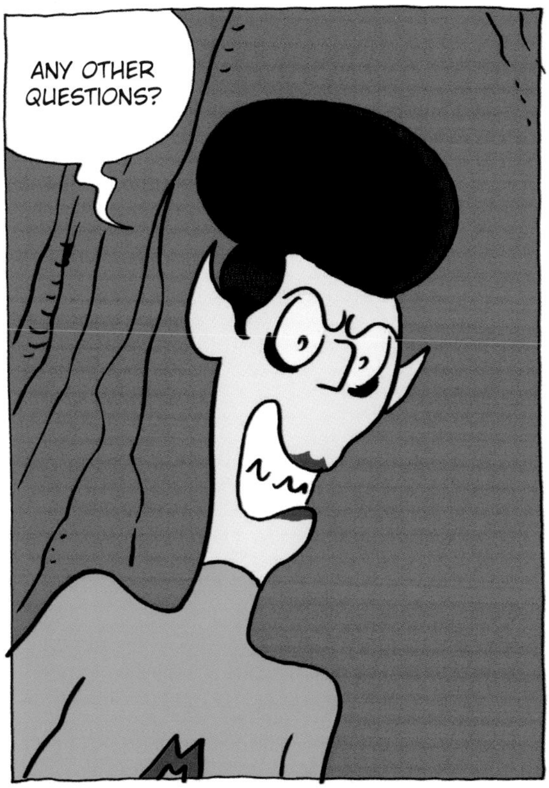
ANY OTHER QUESTIONS?

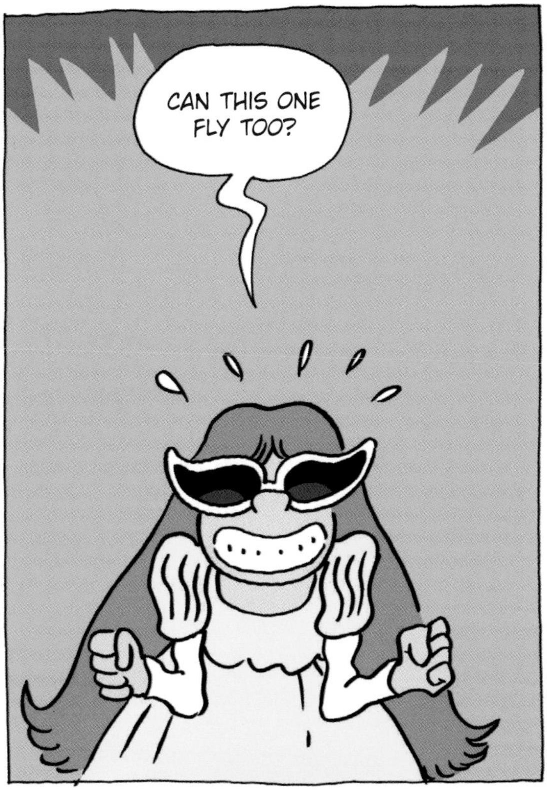
CAN THIS ONE FLY TOO?

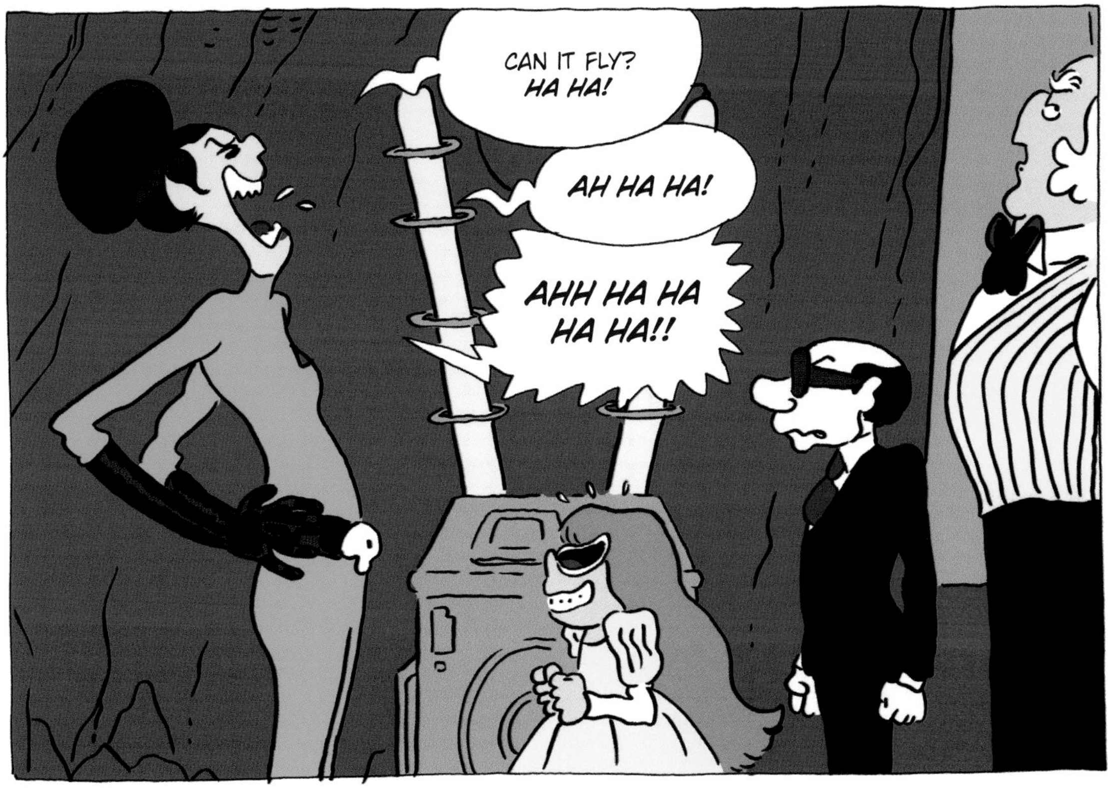
CAN IT FLY? *HA HA!*
AH HA HA!
AHH HA HA HA HA!!

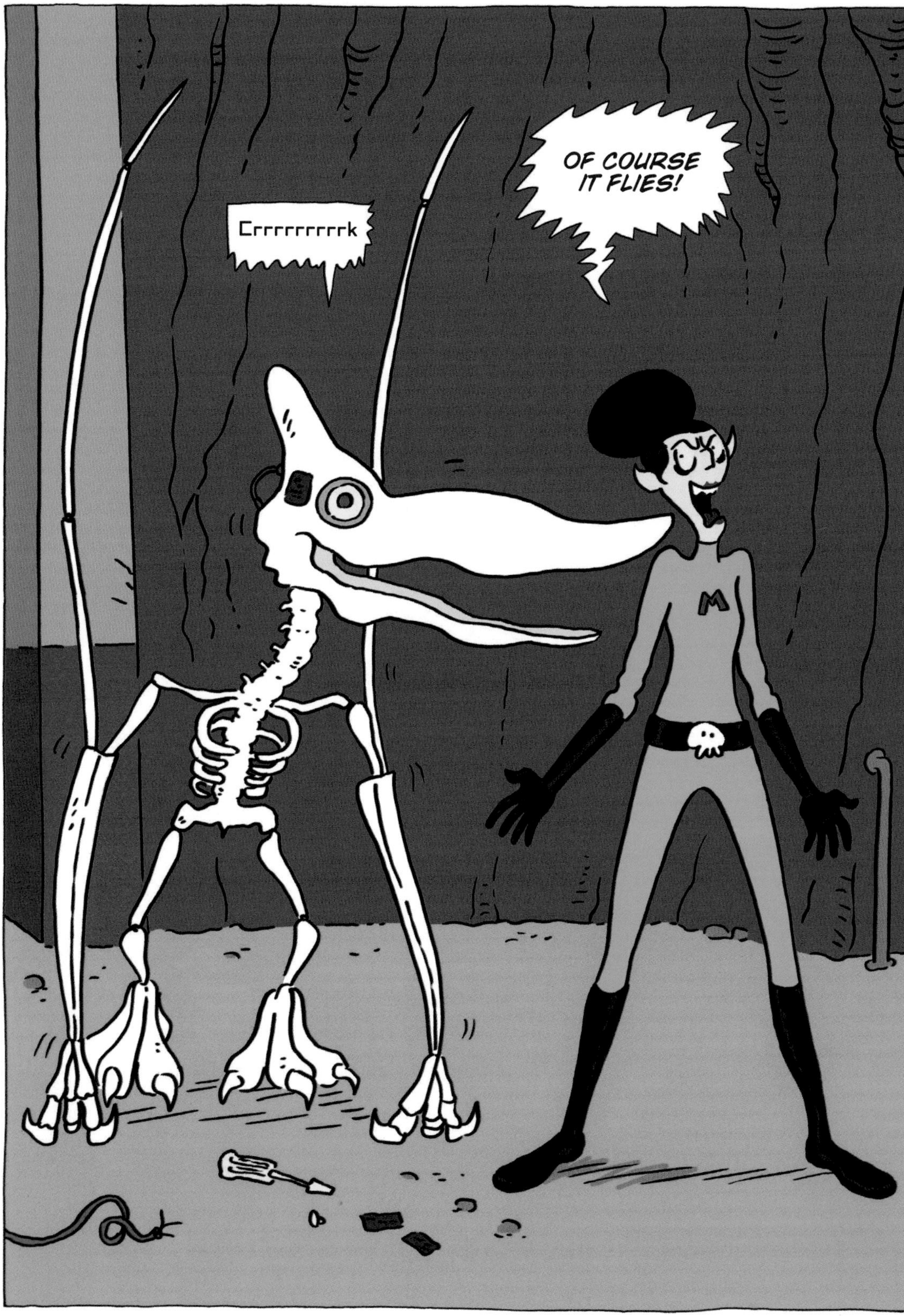
Crrrrrrrrrk
OF COURSE IT FLIES!

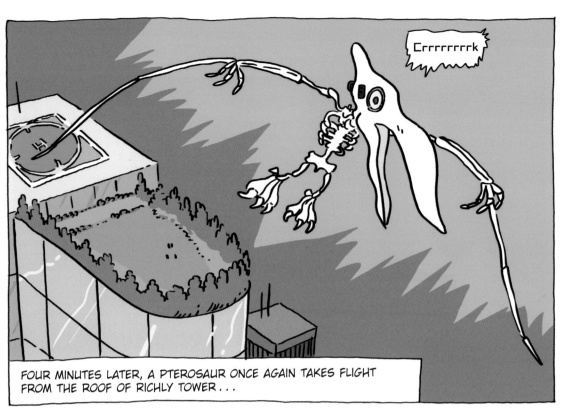

Crrrrrrrrk

FOUR MINUTES LATER, A PTEROSAUR ONCE AGAIN TAKES FLIGHT FROM THE ROOF OF RICHLY TOWER...

FLY, FLY FLY!

HA HA HA HA HA!

SIGH...

I DON'T WANT ANY MORE PTEROSAURS.

I'M BORED.

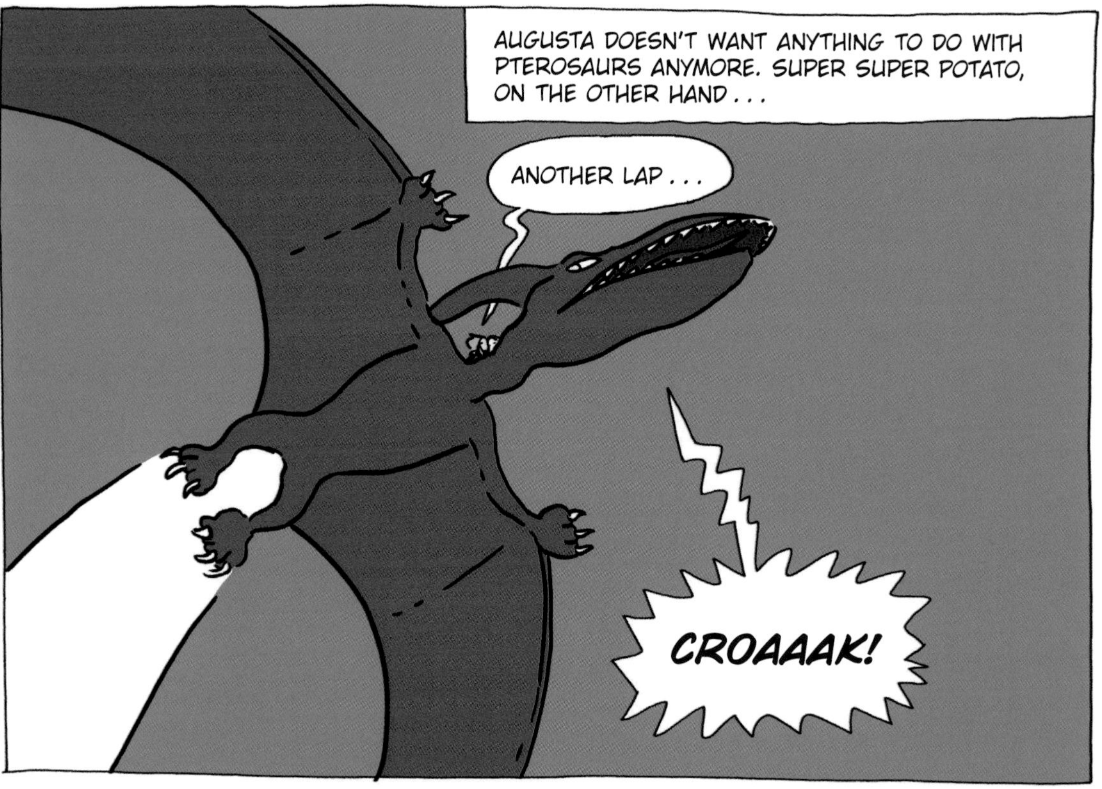
AUGUSTA DOESN'T WANT ANYTHING TO DO WITH PTEROSAURS ANYMORE. SUPER SUPER POTATO, ON THE OTHER HAND . . .
ANOTHER LAP . . .
CROAAAK!

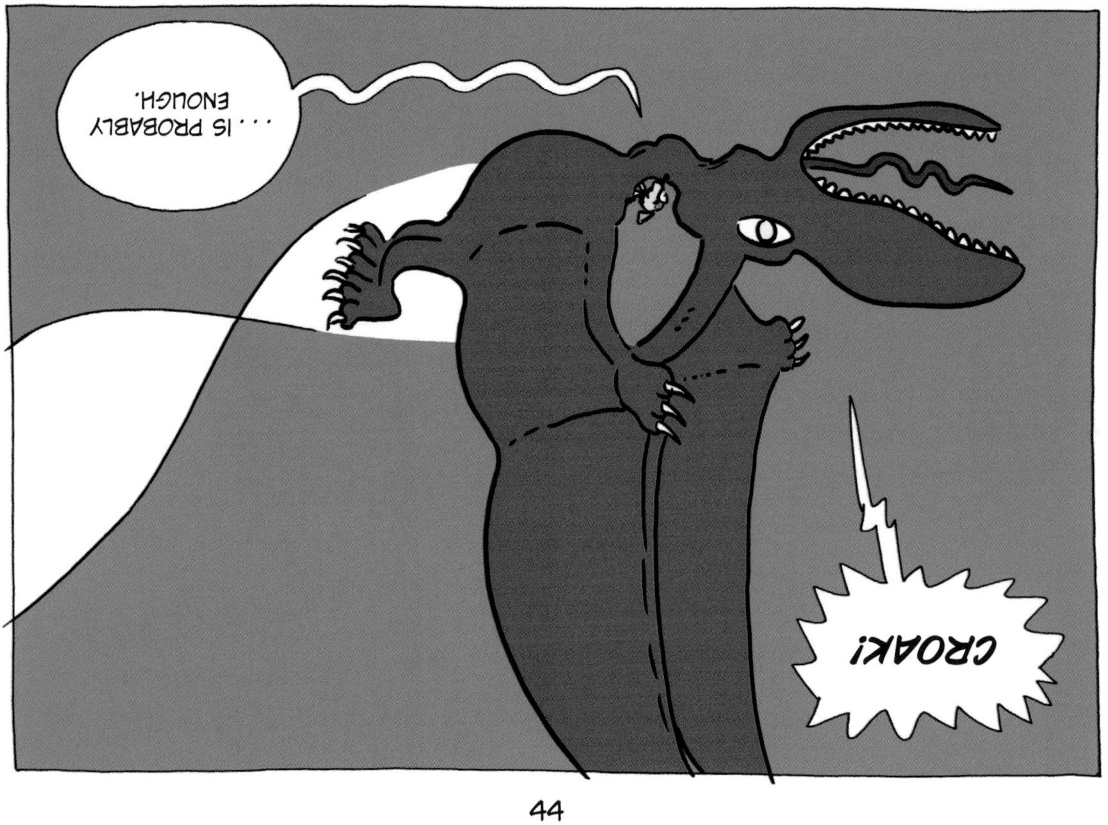
. . . IS PROBABLY ENOUGH.
CROAK!

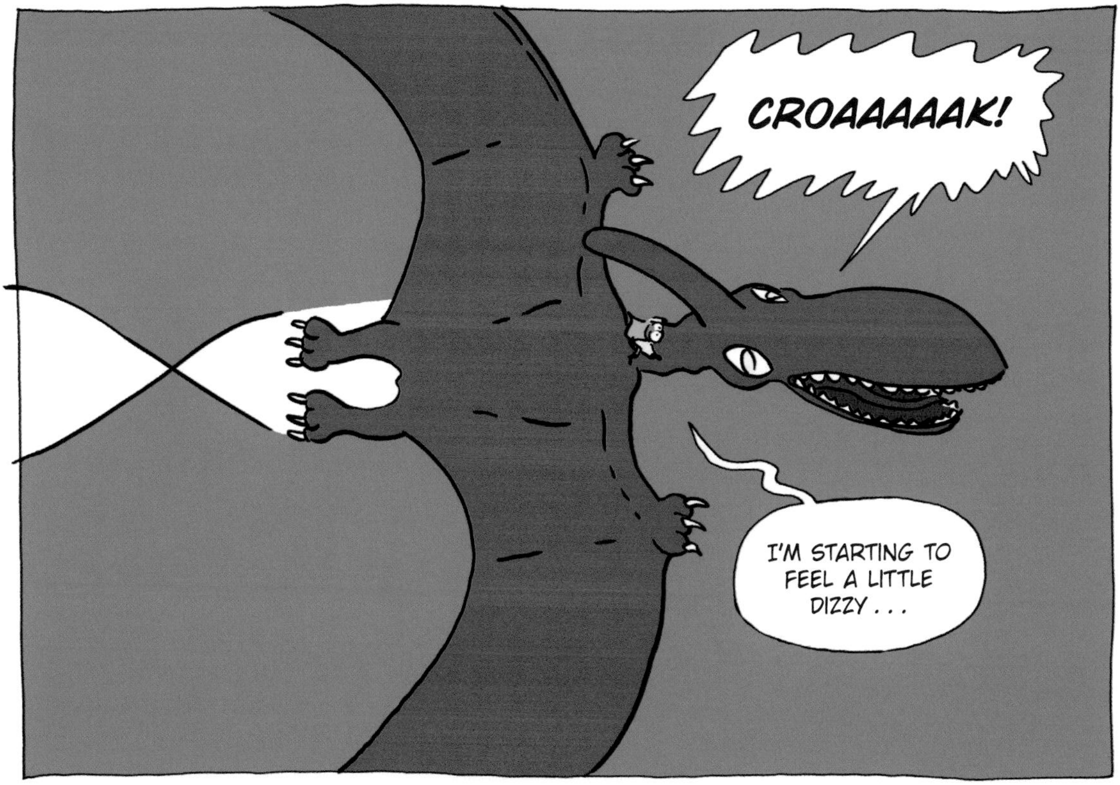
CROAAAAAK!
I'M STARTING TO FEEL A LITTLE DIZZY . . .

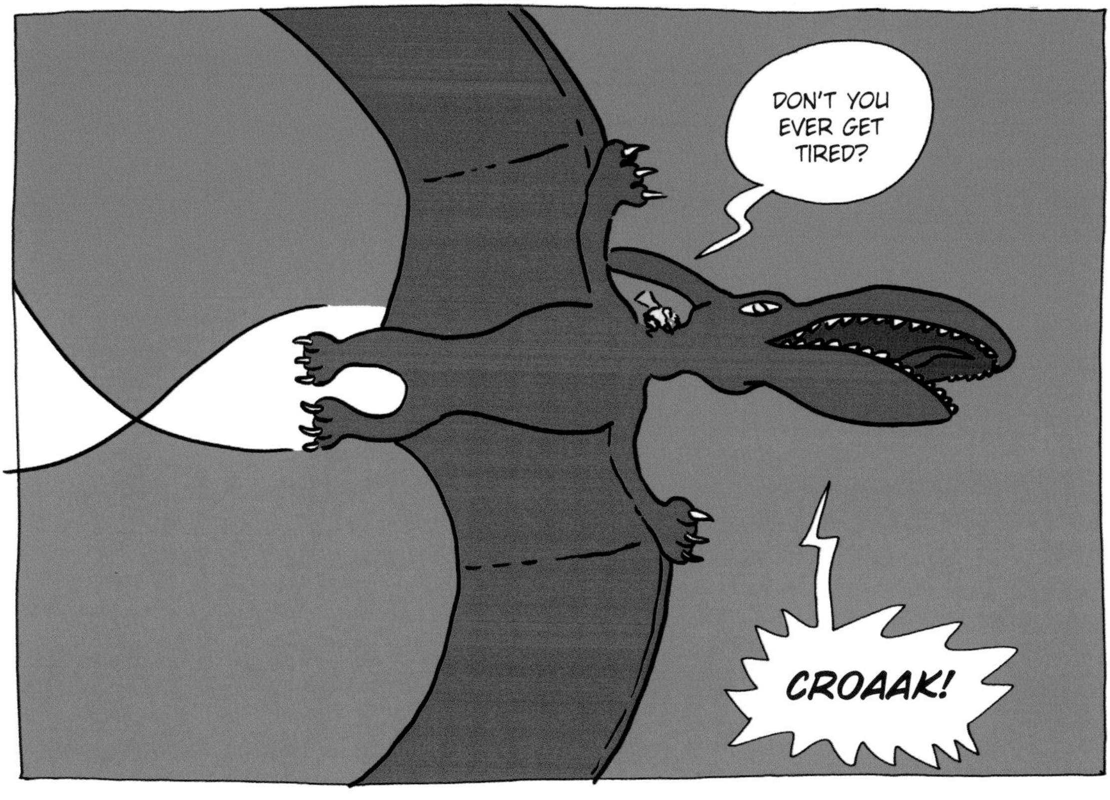
DON'T YOU EVER GET TIRED?
CROAAK!

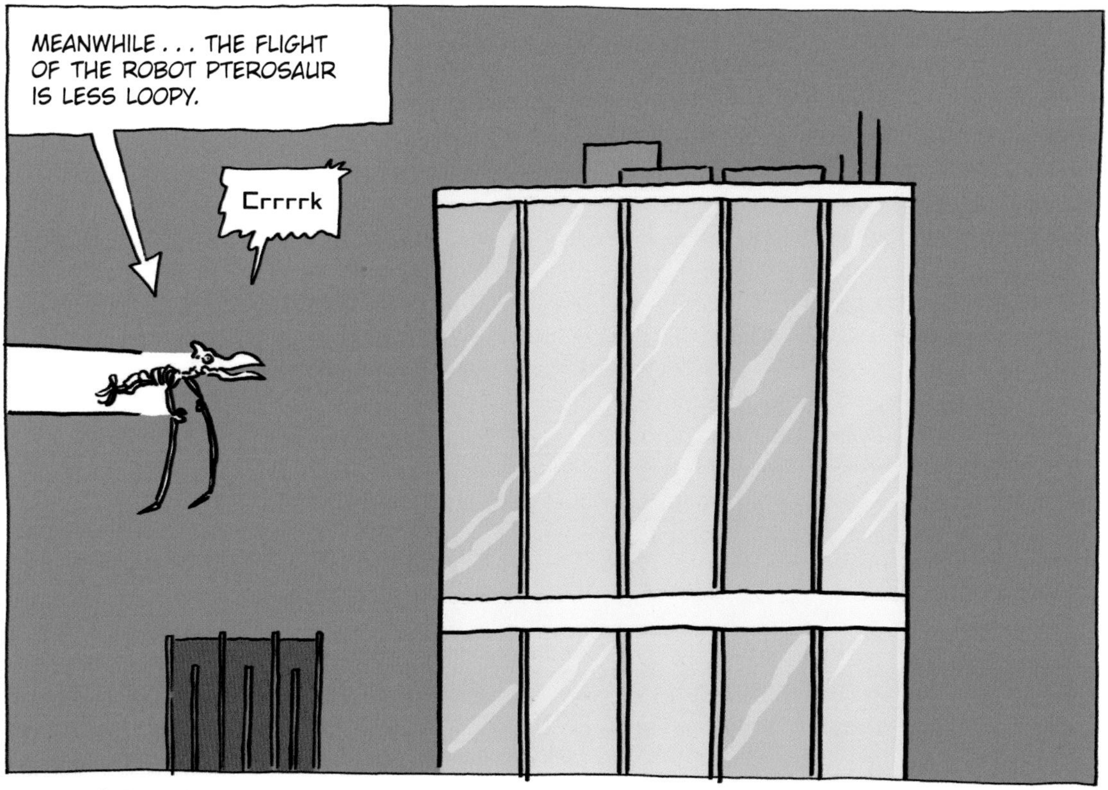
MEANWHILE . . . THE FLIGHT OF THE ROBOT PTEROSAUR IS LESS LOOPY.
Crrrrk

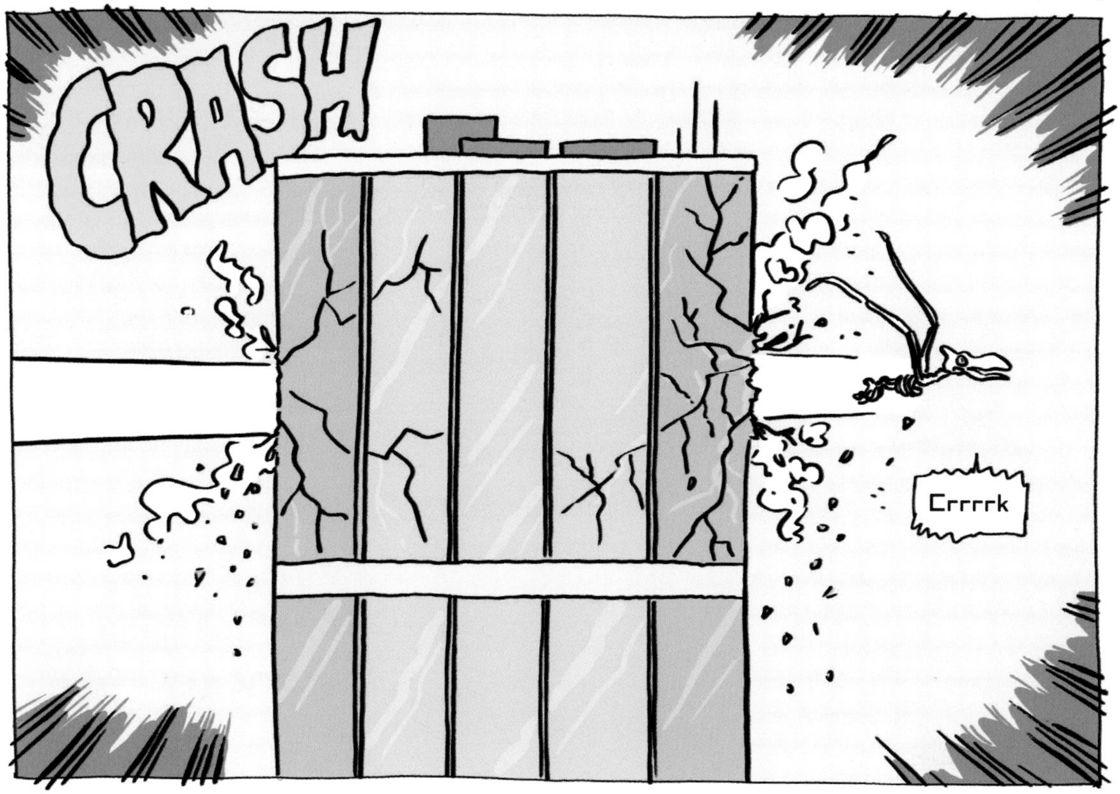
CRASH
Crrrrk

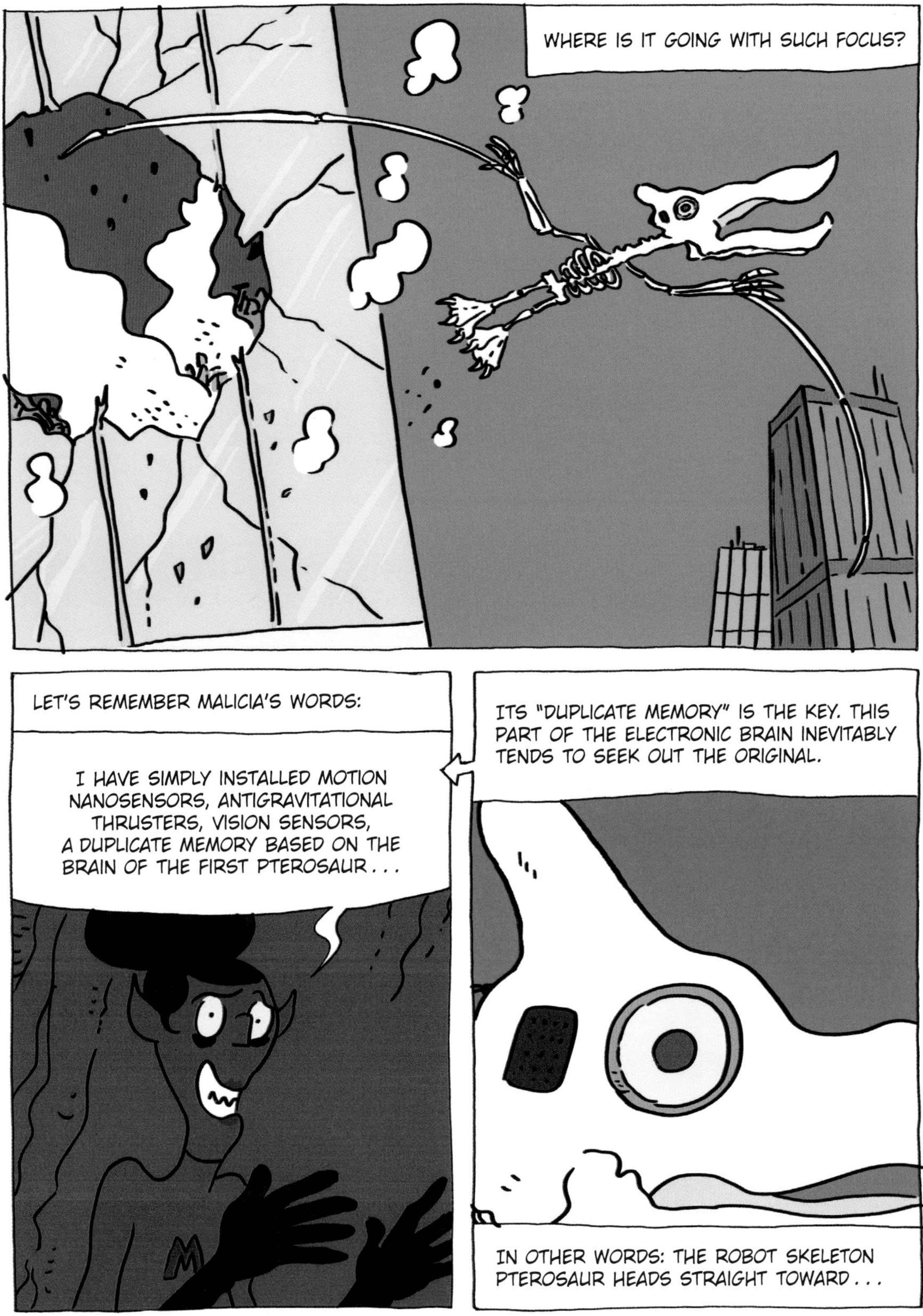
WHERE IS IT GOING WITH SUCH FOCUS?
LET'S REMEMBER MALICIA'S WORDS:
I HAVE SIMPLY INSTALLED MOTION NANOSENSORS, ANTIGRAVITATIONAL THRUSTERS, VISION SENSORS, A DUPLICATE MEMORY BASED ON THE BRAIN OF THE FIRST PTEROSAUR . . .
ITS "DUPLICATE MEMORY" IS THE KEY. THIS PART OF THE ELECTRONIC BRAIN INEVITABLY TENDS TO SEEK OUT THE ORIGINAL.
IN OTHER WORDS: THE ROBOT SKELETON PTEROSAUR HEADS STRAIGHT TOWARD . . .

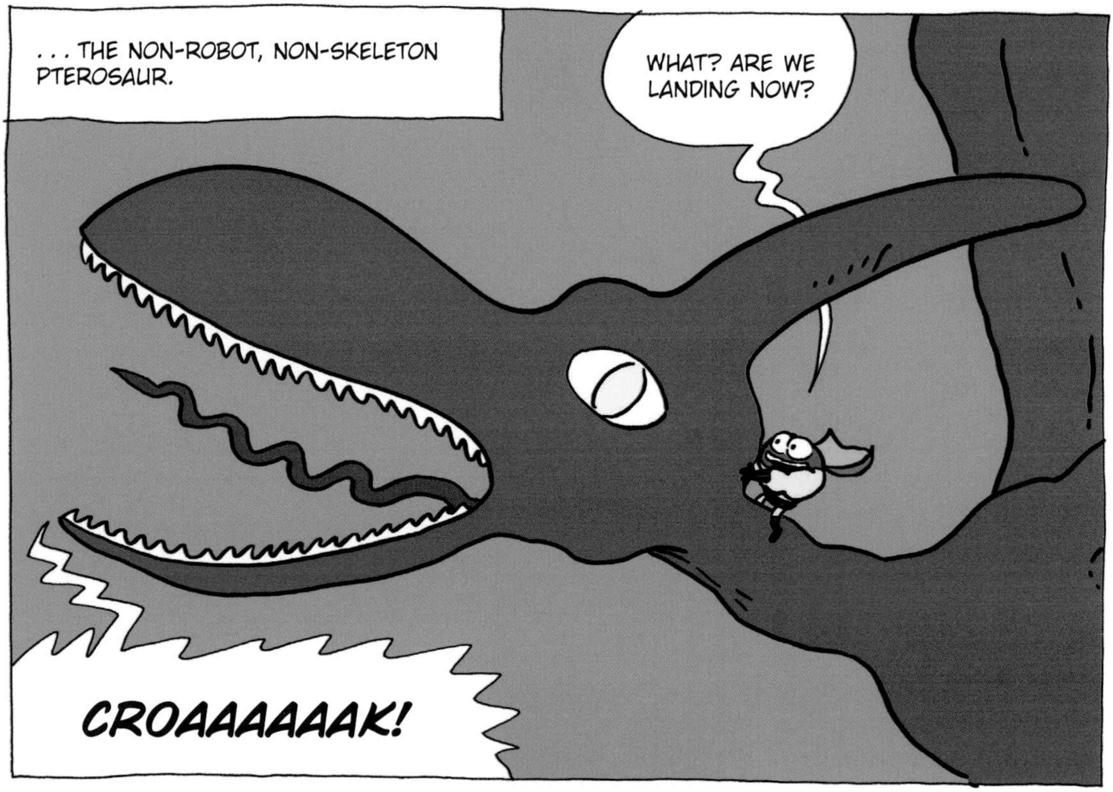
. . . THE NON-ROBOT, NON-SKELETON PTEROSAUR.
WHAT? ARE WE LANDING NOW?
CROAAAAAAK!

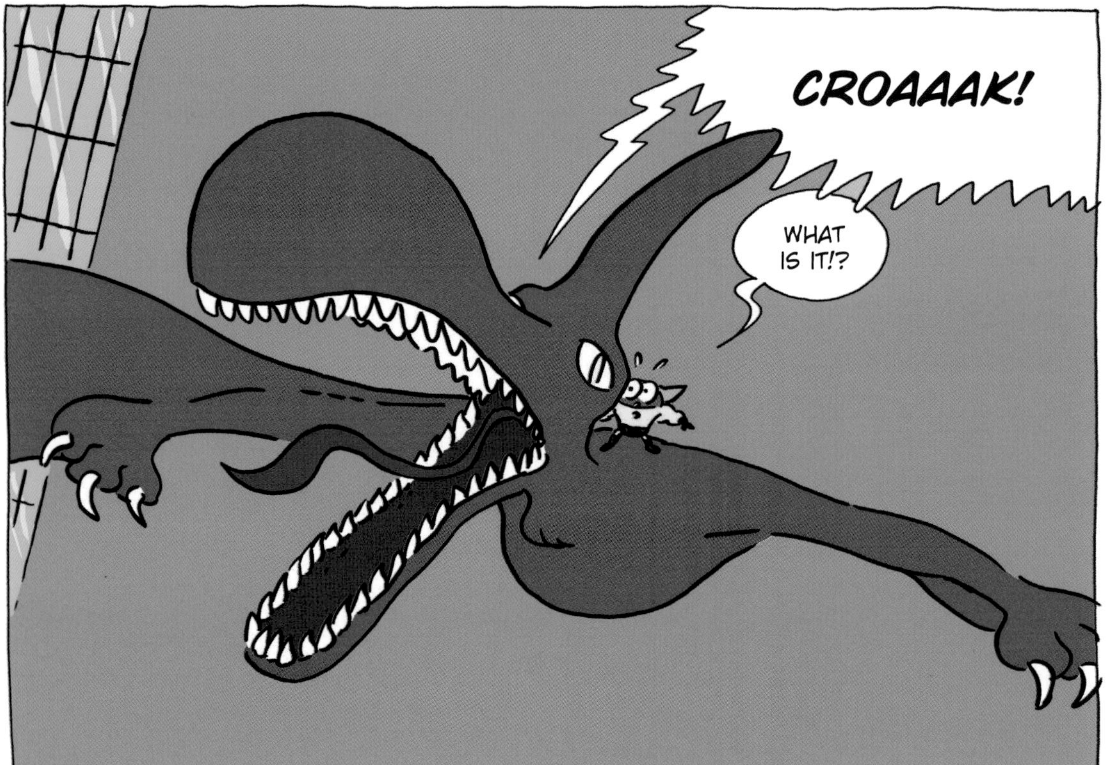
CROAAAK!
WHAT IS IT!?

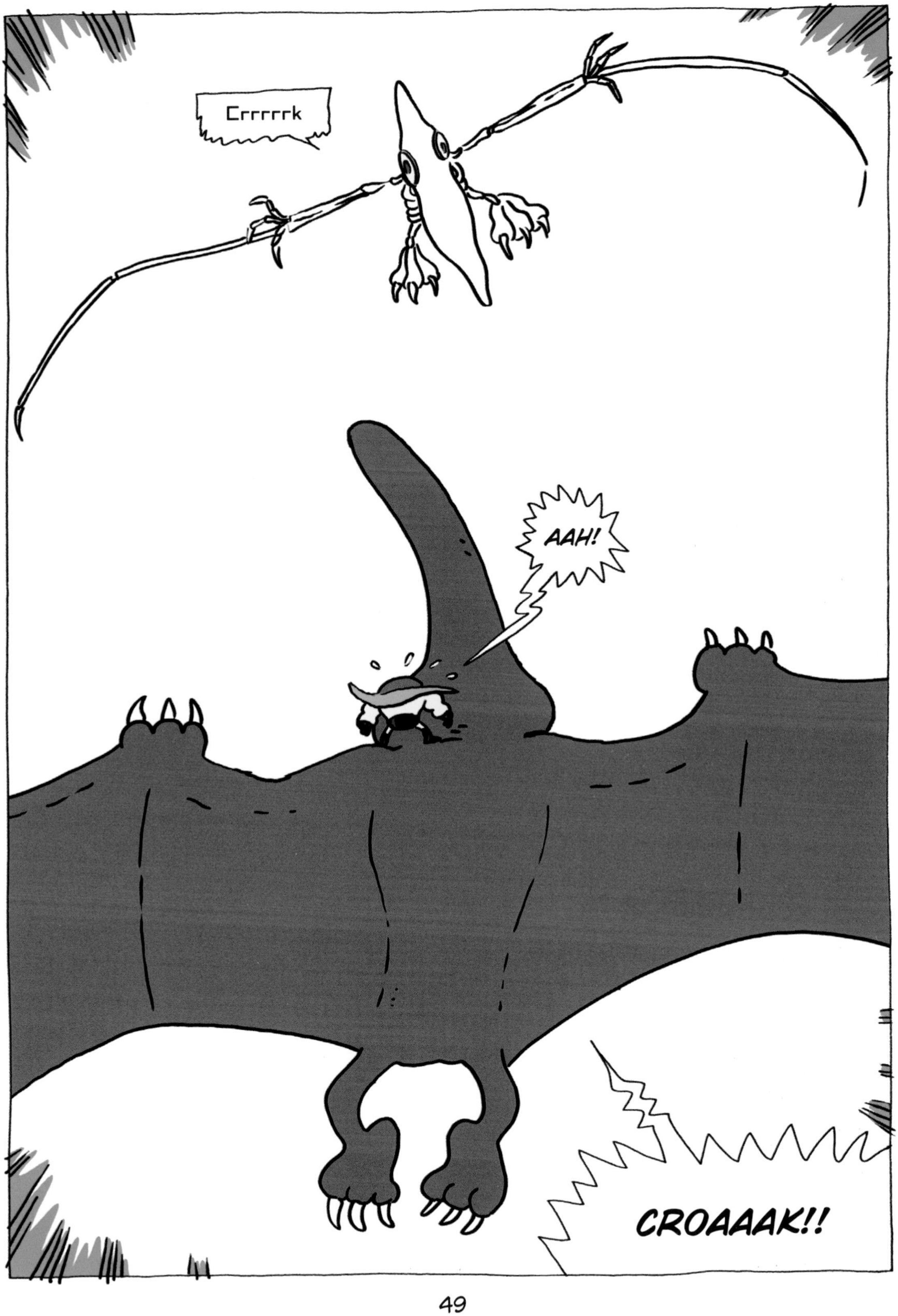

Crrrrrk
AAH!
CROAAAK!!

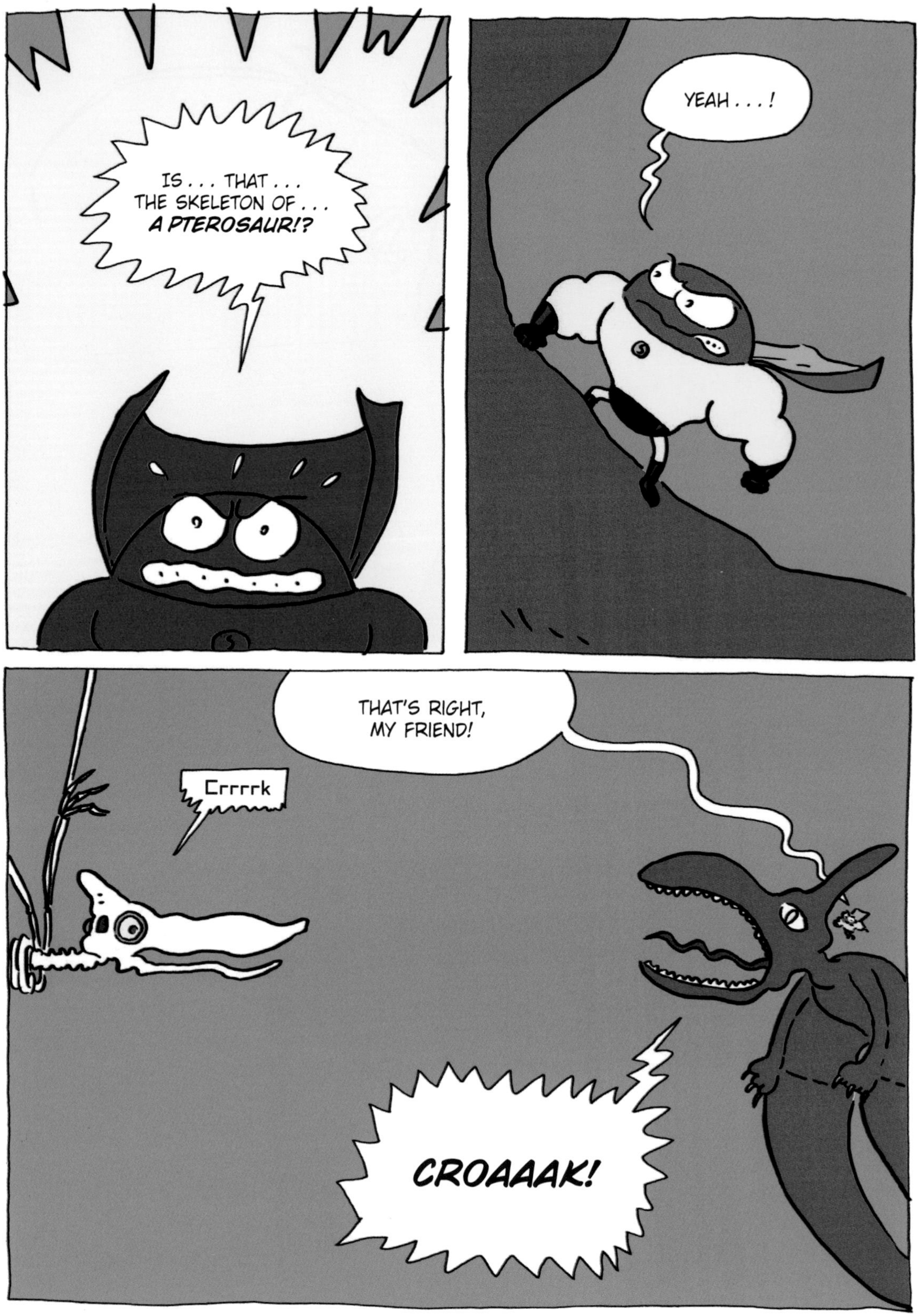
IS . . . THAT . . .
THE SKELETON OF . . .
A PTEROSAUR!?
YEAH . . . !
THAT'S RIGHT,
MY FRIEND!
Crrrrk
CROAAAK!

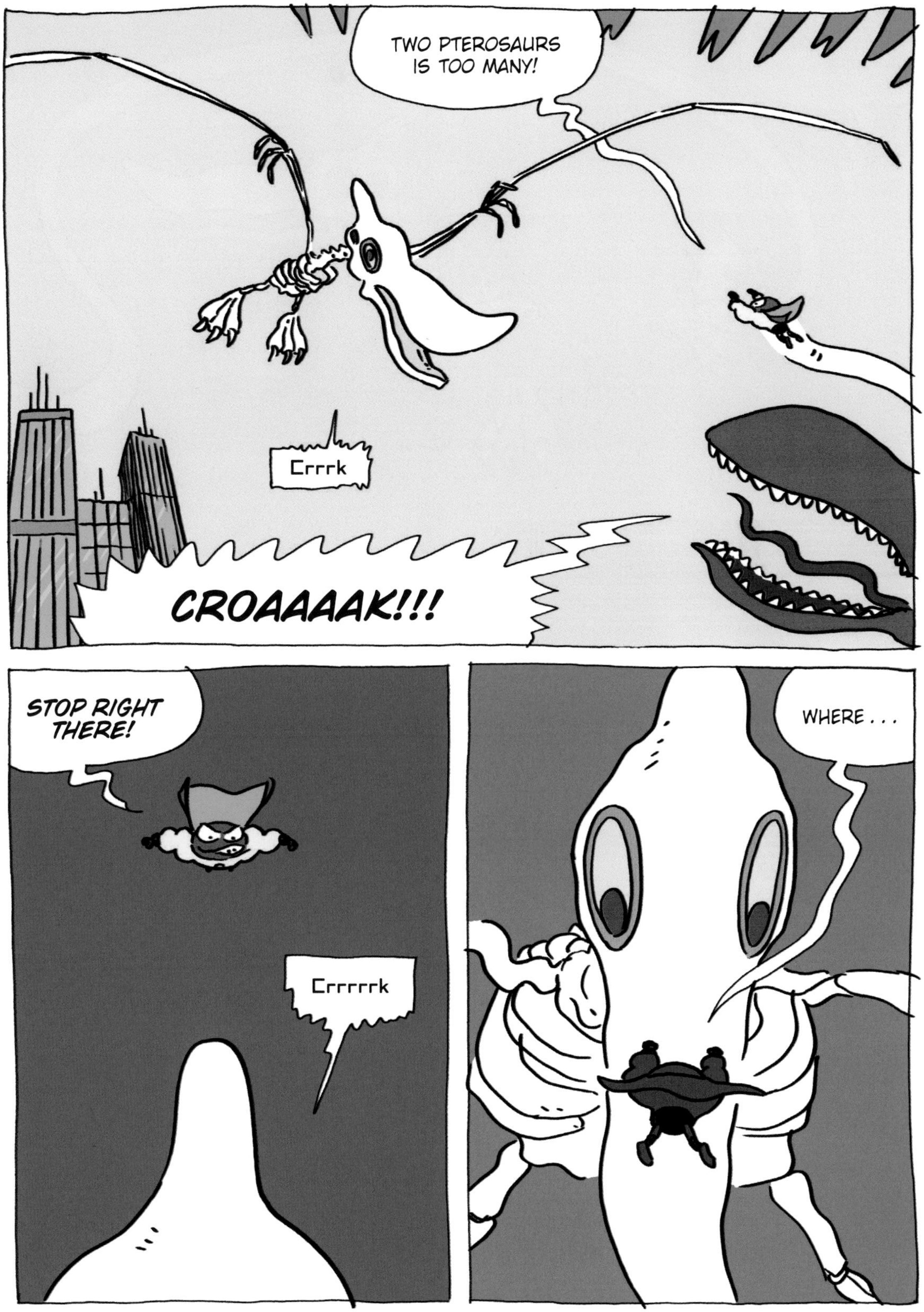
TWO PTEROSAURS IS TOO MANY!
Crrrk
CROAAAAK!!!
STOP RIGHT THERE!
Crrrrrk
WHERE . . .

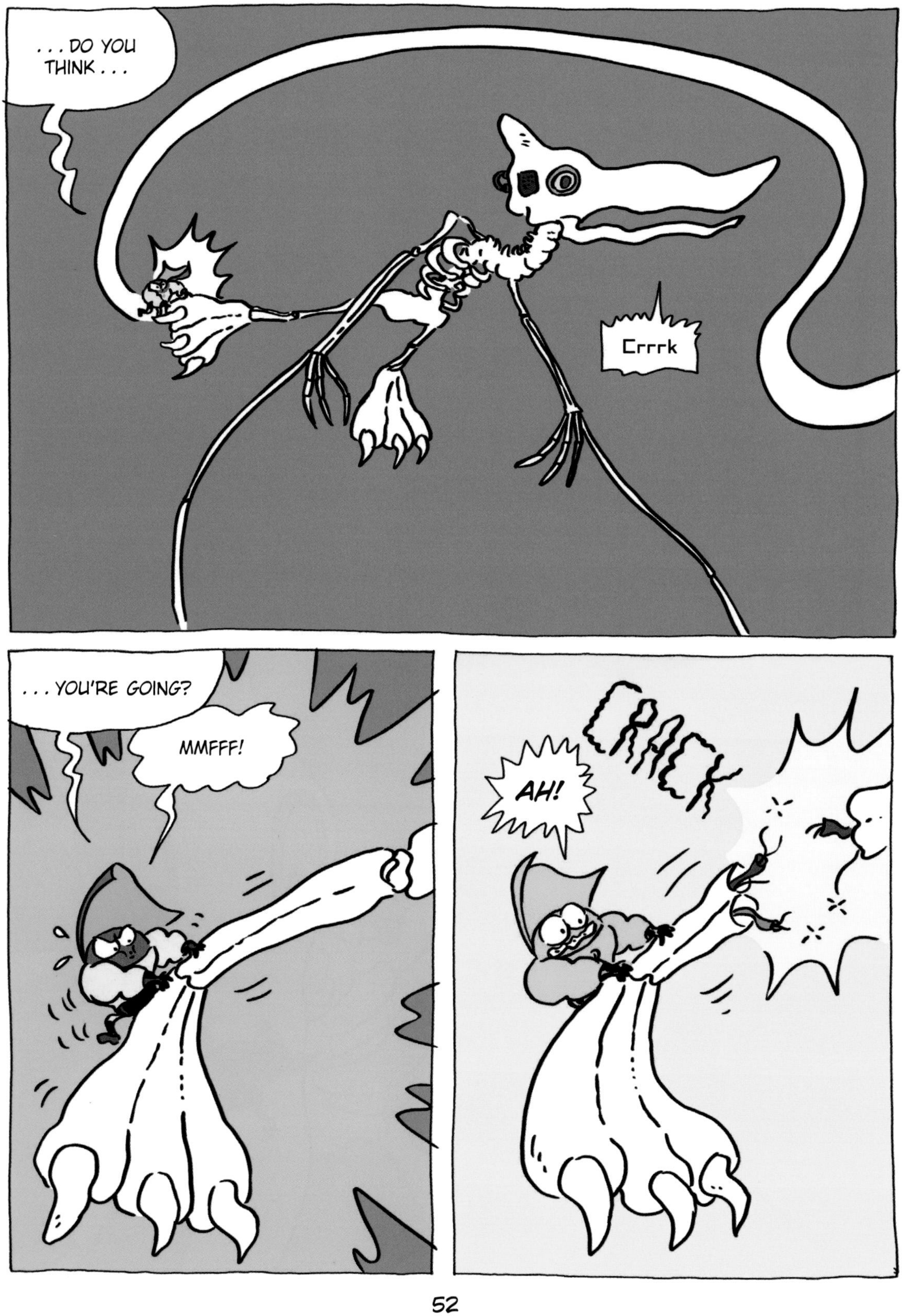
. . . DO YOU THINK . . .
Crrrk
. . . YOU'RE GOING?
MMFFF!
CRACK
AH!

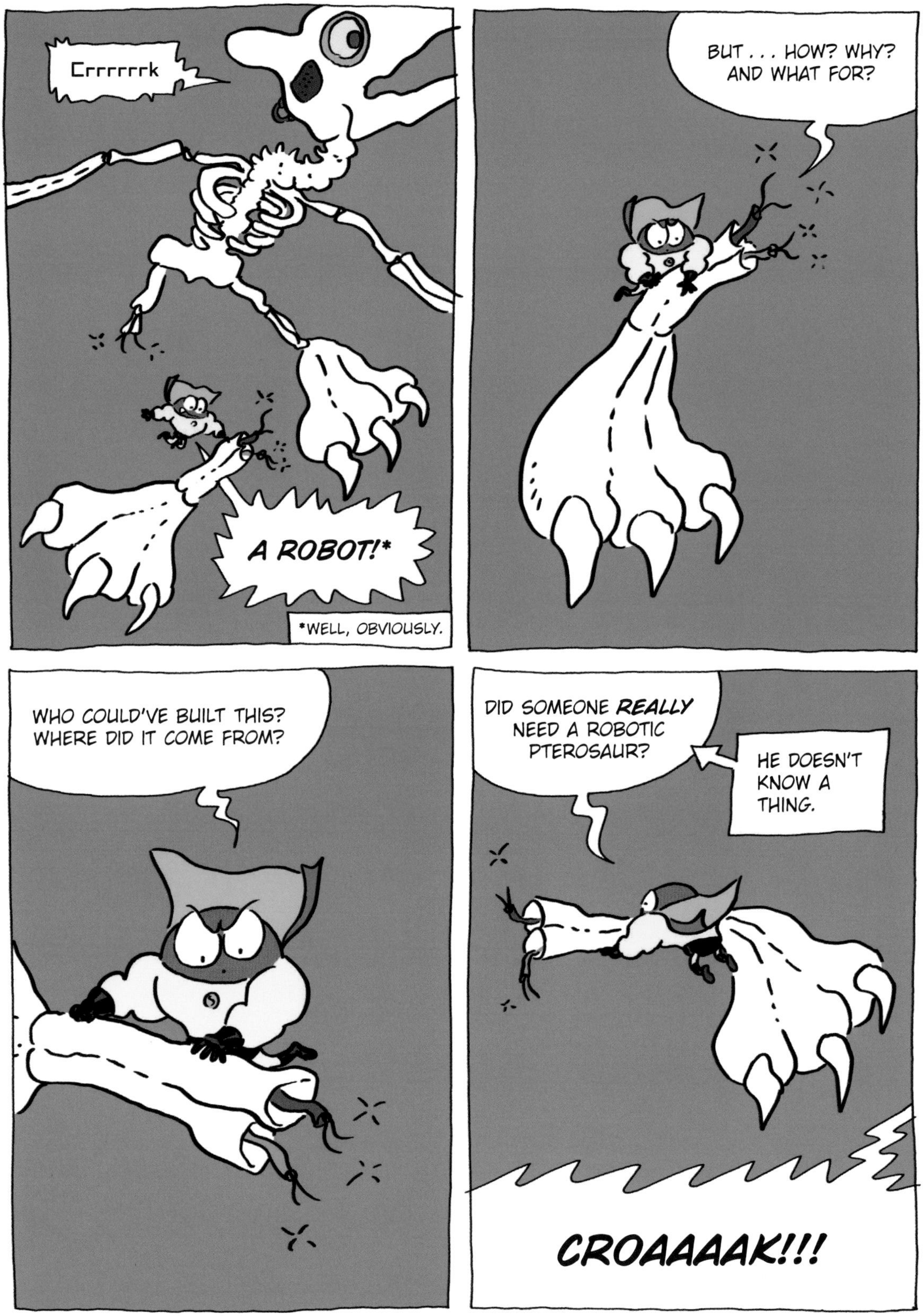
Crrrrrrk
A ROBOT!*
*WELL, OBVIOUSLY.
BUT . . . HOW? WHY? AND WHAT FOR?
WHO COULD'VE BUILT THIS? WHERE DID IT COME FROM?
DID SOMEONE ***REALLY*** NEED A ROBOTIC PTEROSAUR?
HE DOESN'T KNOW A THING.
CROAAAAK!!!

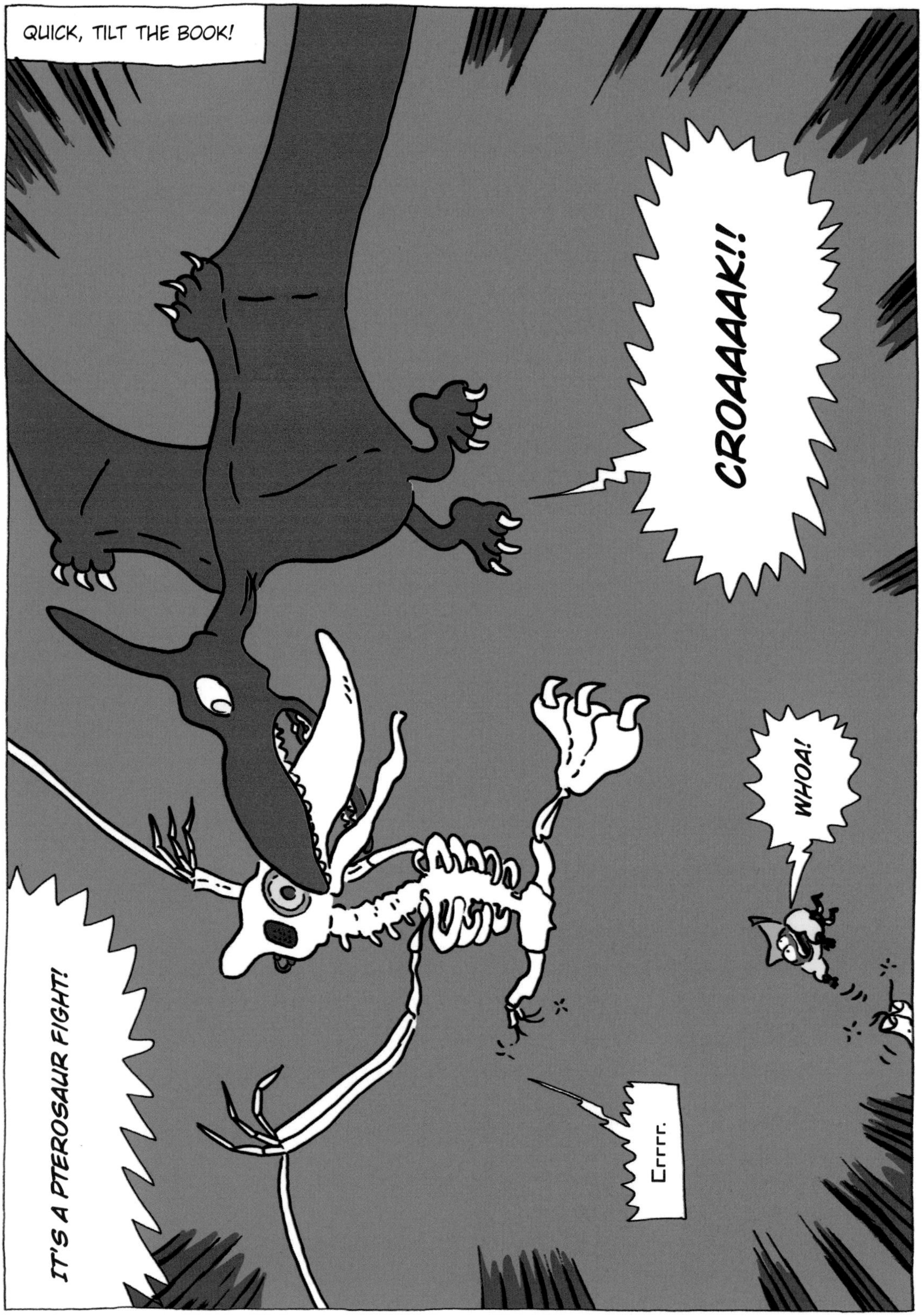
QUICK, TILT THE BOOK!
IT'S A PTEROSAUR FIGHT!
Crrrr.
CROAAAAK!!
WHOA!

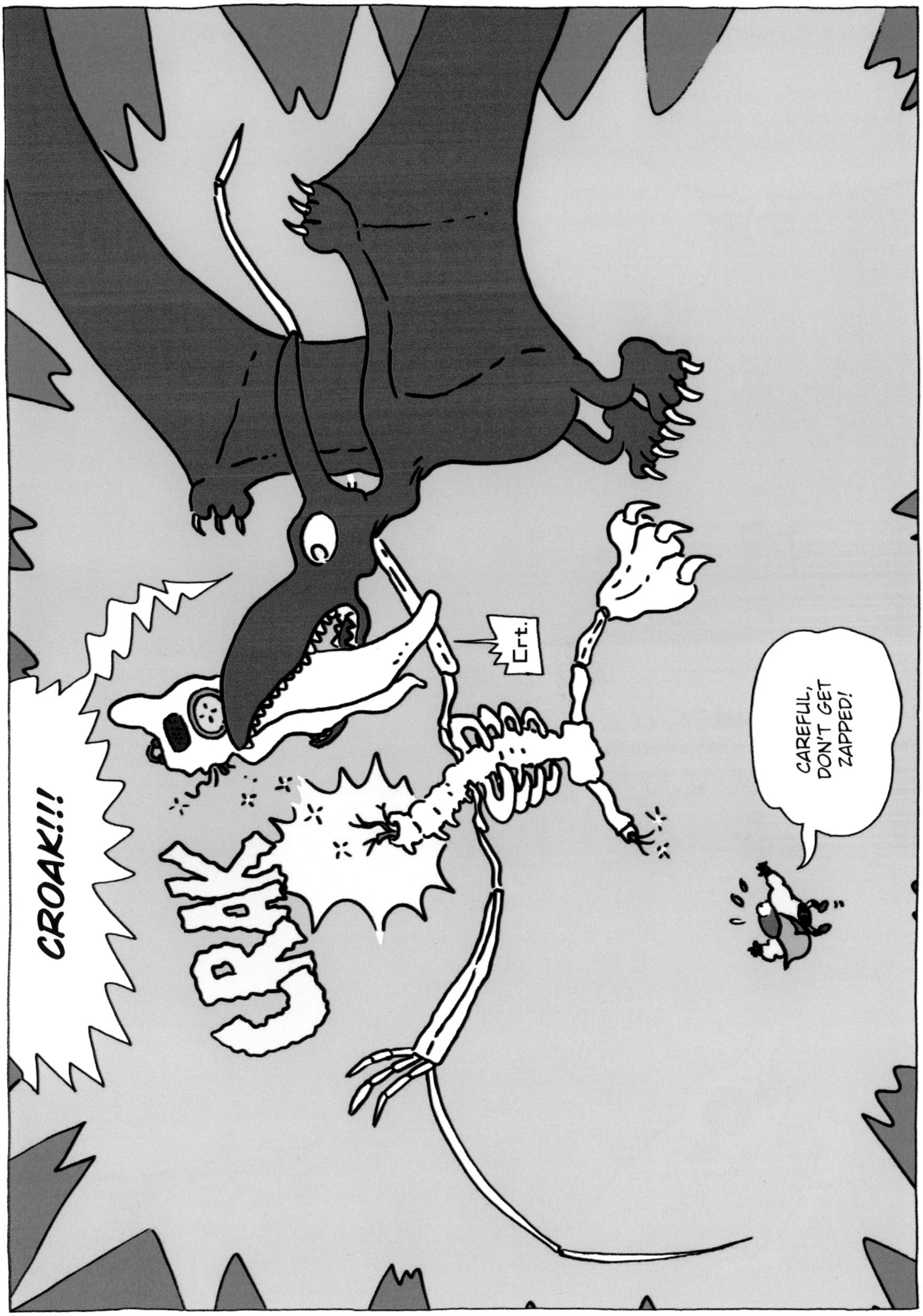
CROAK!!!
CRAK
Crt.
CAREFUL, DON'T GET ZAPPED!

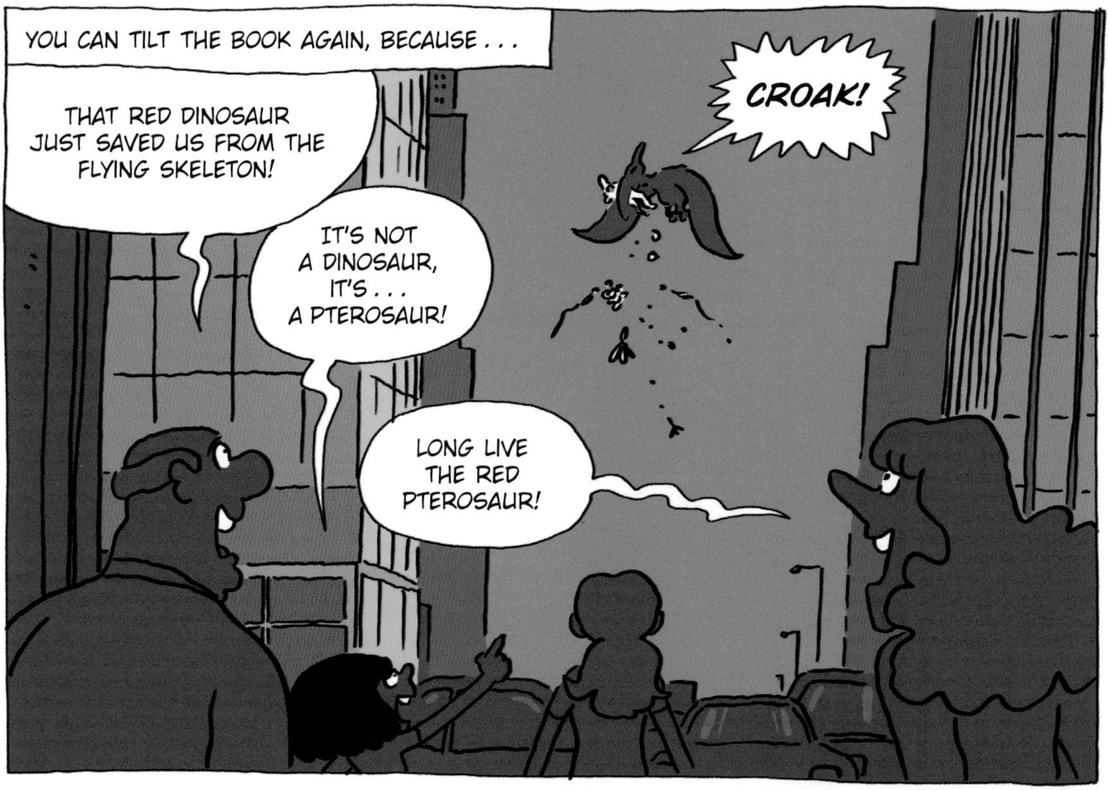
YOU CAN TILT THE BOOK AGAIN, BECAUSE . . .
THAT RED DINOSAUR JUST SAVED US FROM THE FLYING SKELETON!
CROAK!
IT'S NOT A DINOSAUR, IT'S . . . A PTEROSAUR!
LONG LIVE THE RED PTEROSAUR!

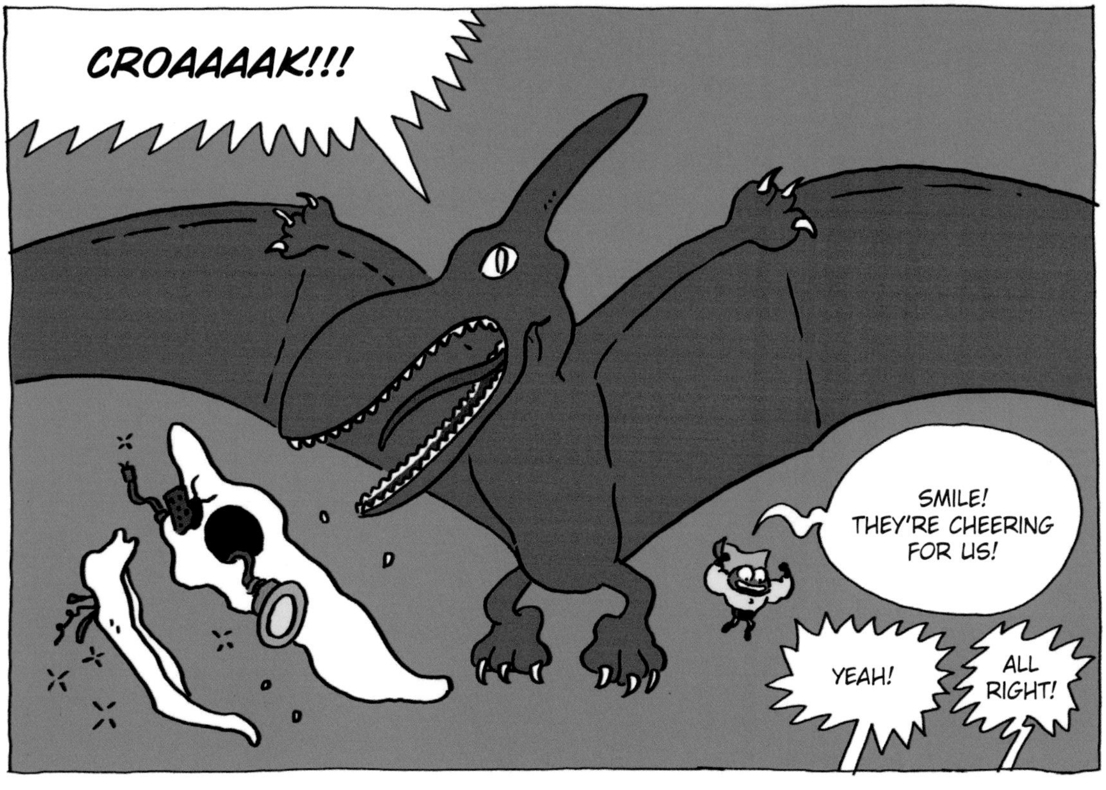
CROAAAAK!!!
SMILE! THEY'RE CHEERING FOR US!
YEAH!
ALL RIGHT!

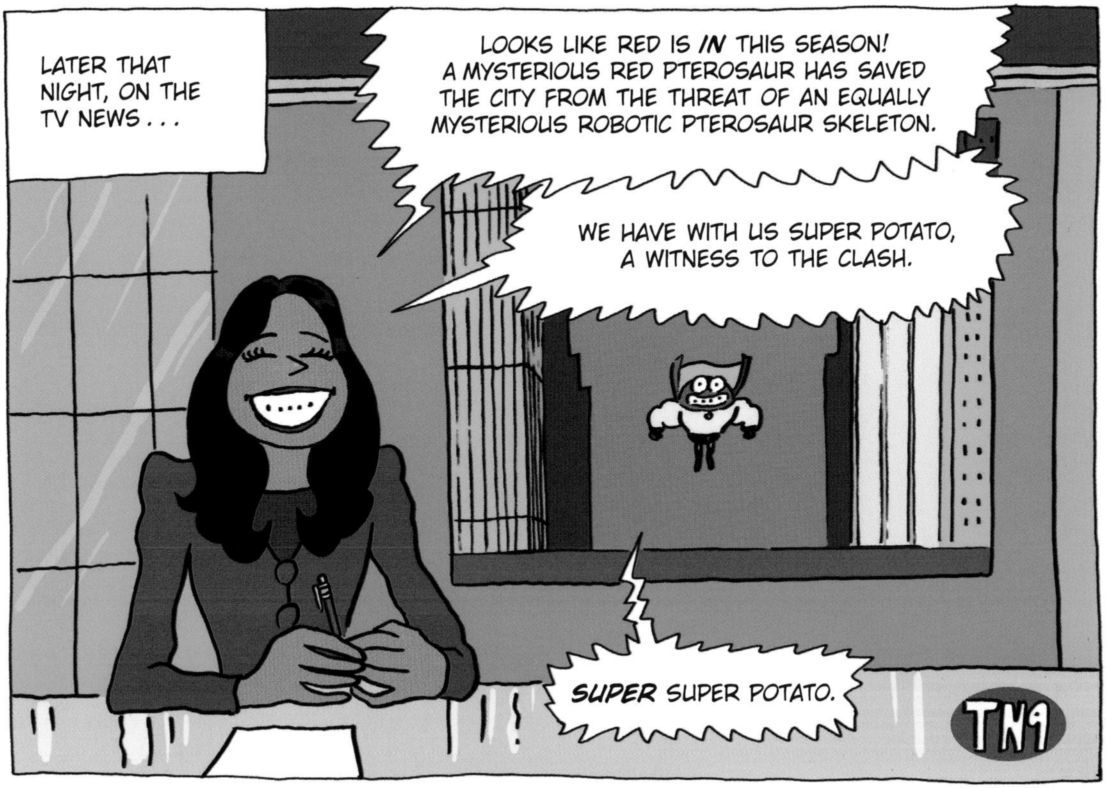
LATER THAT NIGHT, ON THE TV NEWS . . .
LOOKS LIKE RED IS *IN* THIS SEASON! A MYSTERIOUS RED PTEROSAUR HAS SAVED THE CITY FROM THE THREAT OF AN EQUALLY MYSTERIOUS ROBOTIC PTEROSAUR SKELETON.
WE HAVE WITH US SUPER POTATO, A WITNESS TO THE CLASH.
SUPER SUPER POTATO.
TN9

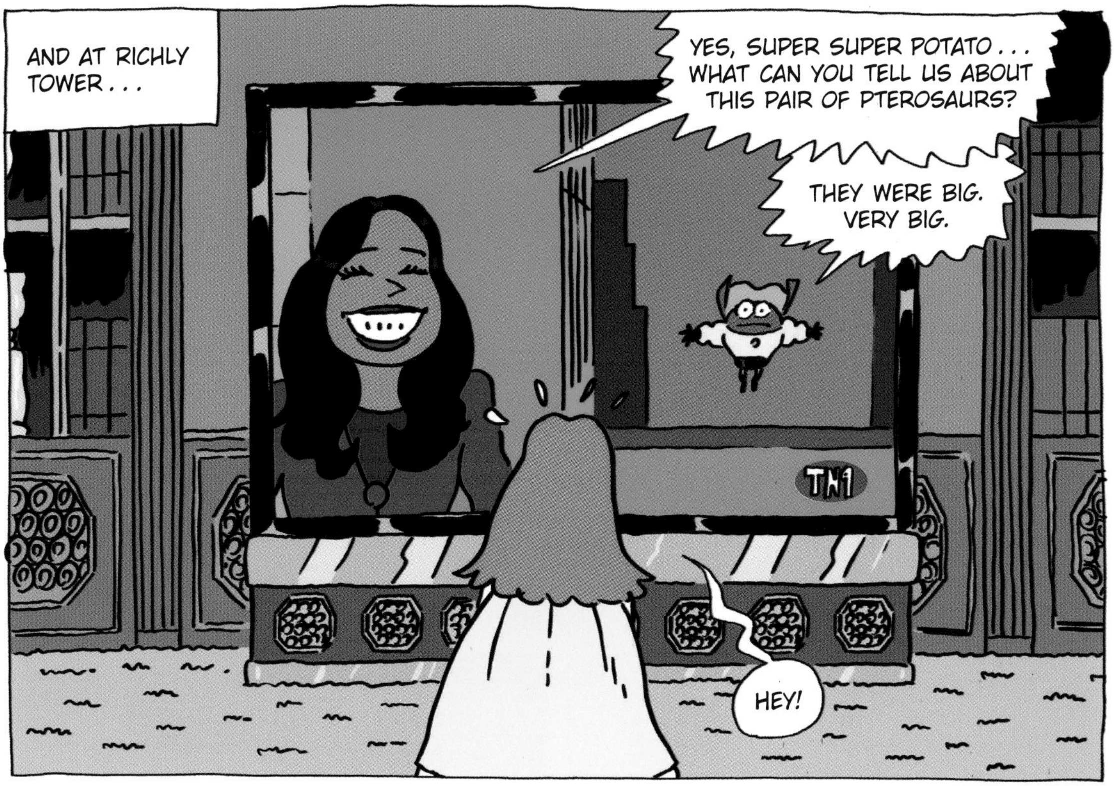
AND AT RICHLY TOWER . . .
YES, SUPER SUPER POTATO . . . WHAT CAN YOU TELL US ABOUT THIS PAIR OF PTEROSAURS?
THEY WERE BIG. VERY BIG.
TN9
HEY!

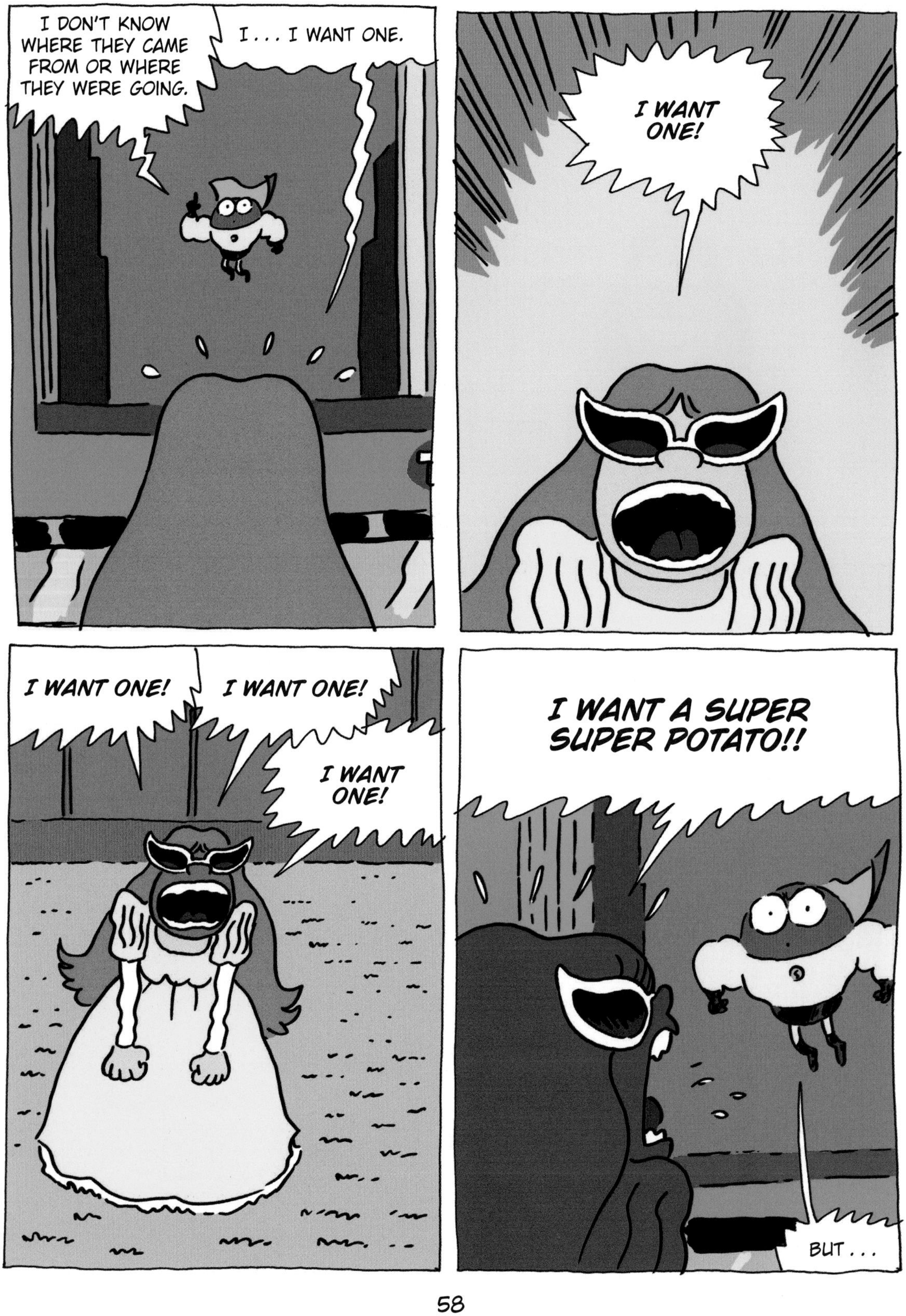
I DON'T KNOW WHERE THEY CAME FROM OR WHERE THEY WERE GOING.
I . . . I WANT ONE.
I WANT ONE!
I WANT ONE!
I WANT ONE!
I WANT ONE!
I WANT A SUPER SUPER POTATO!!
BUT . . .

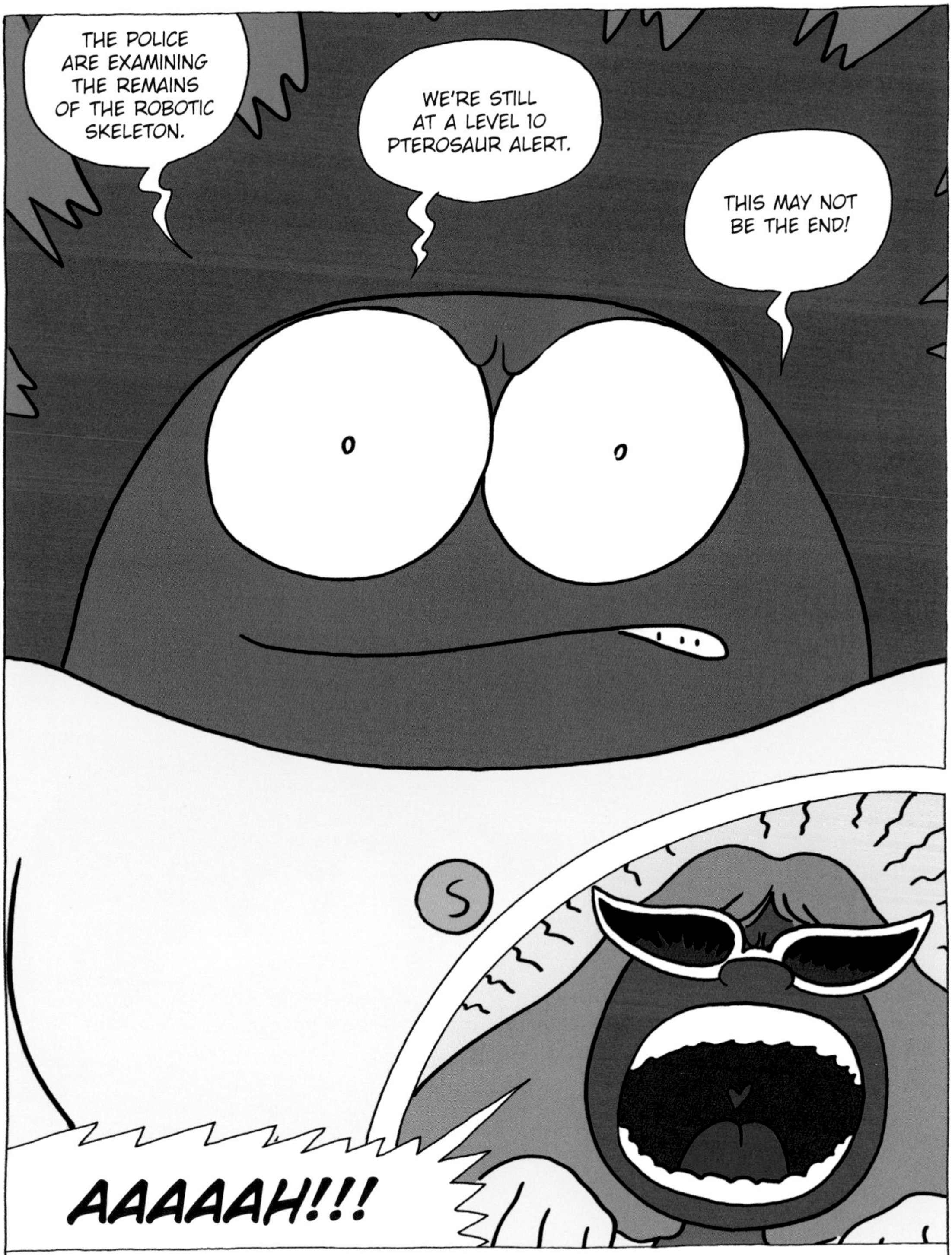
THE POLICE ARE EXAMINING THE REMAINS OF THE ROBOTIC SKELETON.
WE'RE STILL AT A LEVEL 10 PTEROSAUR ALERT.
THIS MAY NOT BE THE END!
AAAAAH!!!

HMM . . . THIS MAY **NOT** BE THE END! WILL SUPER SUPER POTATO DISCOVER THAT THE PTEROSAURS WERE THE LATEST WHIM OF AUGUSTA RICHLY? WILL HE COME FACE-TO-FACE WITH MALICIA THE MALIGNANT ONCE AGAIN? WILL HE END UP THE PET OF THE MOST SPOILED GIRL IN THE WORLD? SO MANY QUESTIONS . . .

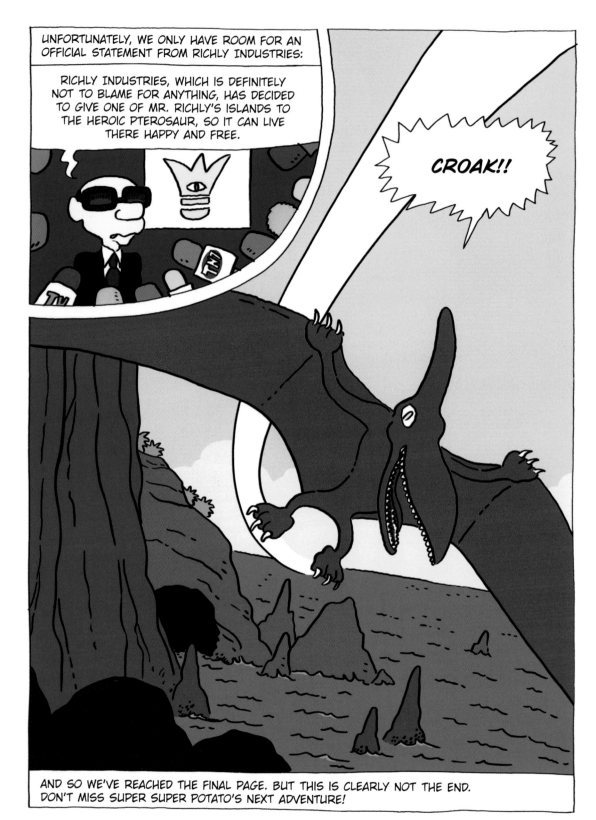

UNFORTUNATELY, WE ONLY HAVE ROOM FOR AN OFFICIAL STATEMENT FROM RICHLY INDUSTRIES:

RICHLY INDUSTRIES, WHICH IS DEFINITELY NOT TO BLAME FOR ANYTHING, HAS DECIDED TO GIVE ONE OF MR. RICHLY'S ISLANDS TO THE HEROIC PTEROSAUR, SO IT CAN LIVE THERE HAPPY AND FREE.

CROAK!!

AND SO WE'VE REACHED THE FINAL PAGE. BUT THIS IS CLEARLY NOT THE END. DON'T MISS SUPER SUPER POTATO'S NEXT ADVENTURE!

For more hilarious tales of Super Potato, check out . . .

SUPER POTATO
#1 THE EPIC ORIGIN OF SUPER POTATO
Artur Laperla

SUPER POTATO
#2 SUPER POTATO'S GALACTIC BREAKOUT
Artur Laperla

SUPER POTATO
#3 SUPER POTATO'S MEGA TIME-TRAVEL ADVENTURE

SUPER POTATO
#4 SUPER POTATO AND THE MUTANT ANIMAL MAYHEM
Artur Laperla

SUPER POTATO
#5 SUPER POTATO AND THE CASTLE OF ROBOTS
Artur Laperla

SUPER POTATO
#6 SUPER POTATO GETS BUFF
Artur Laperla

SUPER POTATO
#7 SUPER POTATO AND THE GREENHOUSE OF EVIL
Artur Laperla

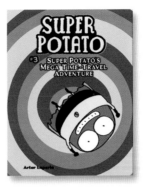

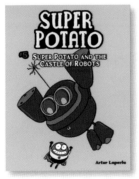

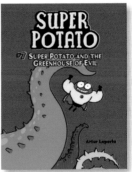

AND TURN THE PAGE FOR A PREVIEW OF OUR HERO'S NEXT ADVENTURE . . .

SUPER POTATO #9

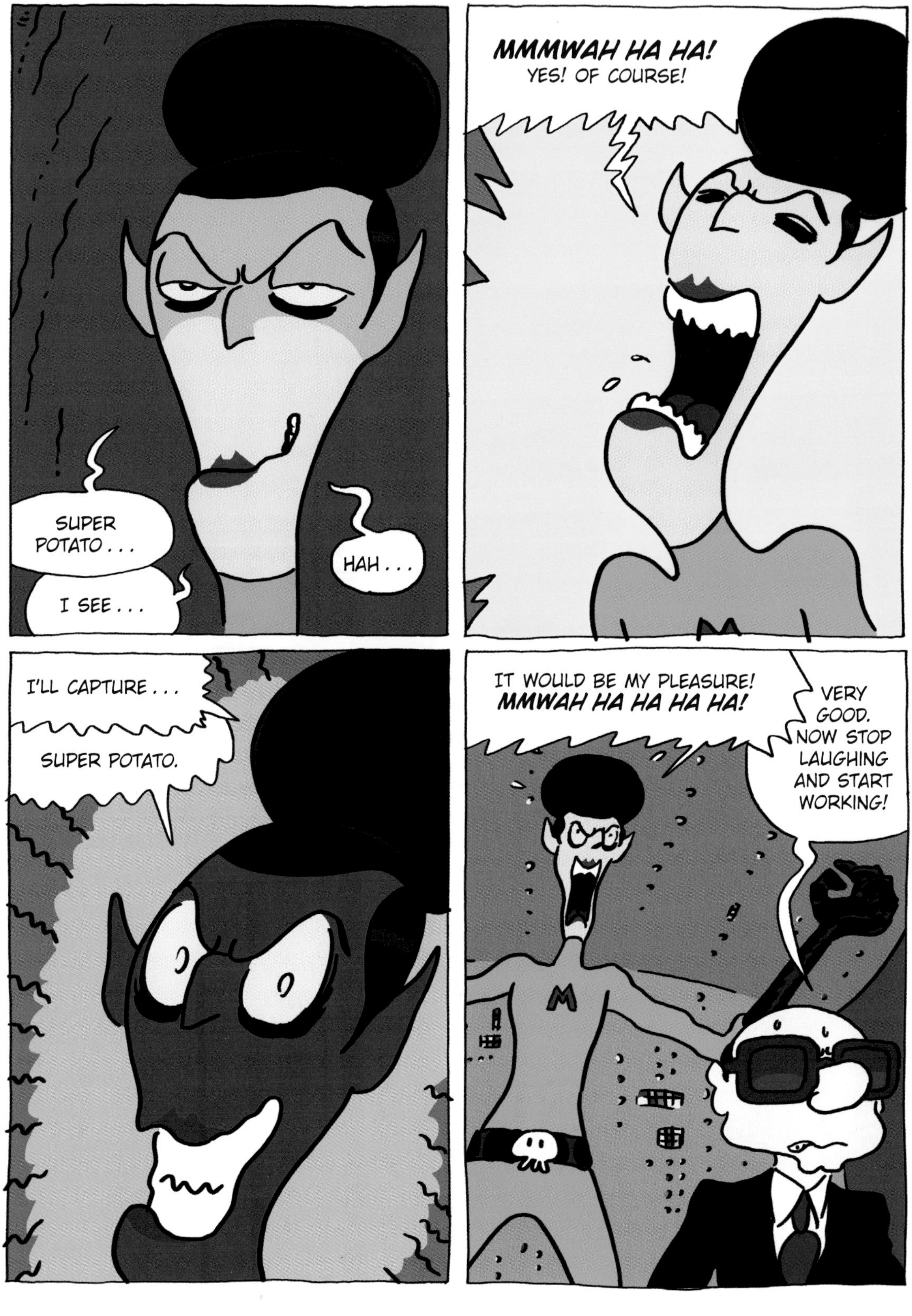
SUPER POTATO . . .
I SEE . . .
HAH . . .
MMMWAH HA HA!
YES! OF COURSE!
I'LL CAPTURE . . .
SUPER POTATO.
IT WOULD BE MY PLEASURE!
MMMWAH HA HA HA HA!
VERY GOOD. NOW STOP LAUGHING AND START WORKING!

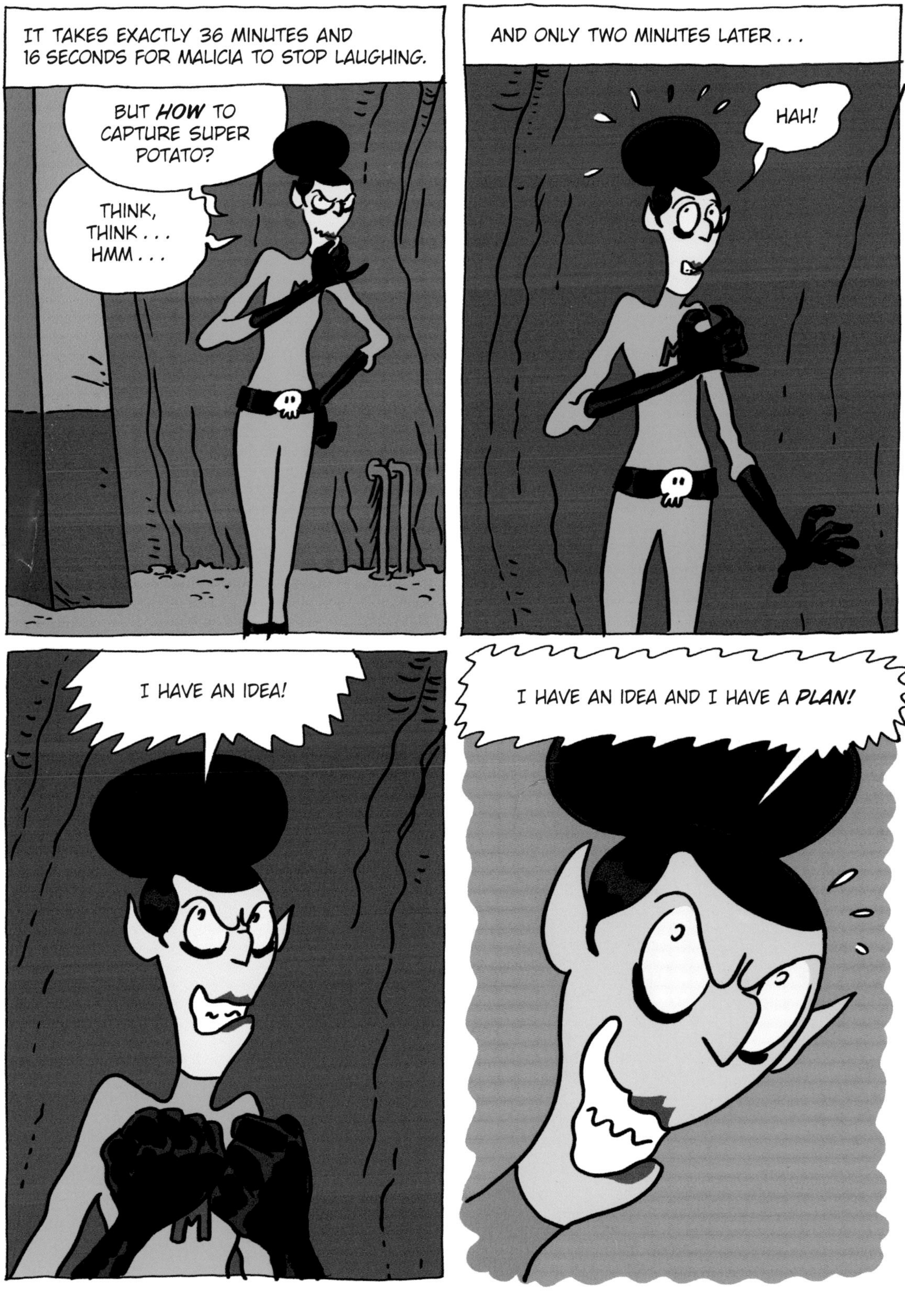
IT TAKES EXACTLY 36 MINUTES AND 16 SECONDS FOR MALICIA TO STOP LAUGHING.
BUT **HOW** TO CAPTURE SUPER POTATO?
THINK, THINK . . . HMM . . .
AND ONLY TWO MINUTES LATER . . .
HAH!
I HAVE AN IDEA!
I HAVE AN IDEA AND I HAVE A **PLAN!**